"It takes effort to know someon[e]

"Then, give me a chance." She tucked in the ragged edges of her pride. "Please give me a second chance."

"One day at a time."

"Can't ask for anything more," Fiona said, knowing that her heart wanted more.

He offered his hand. "Friends."

"To lovers." She shook his hand, afraid that he would withdraw and tuck it behind his back.

"You're quite persuasive."

"We don't have too many days here. Figured that if you wouldn't persuade me, then it's up to me."

"Yeah? Go ahead. Persuade."

Fiona didn't waste another second. She slipped her hands around Leo's neck and tiptoed to reach his mouth.

One kiss. One mouth pressed against the other. That was all it was.

Except when she kissed Leo, she wanted more. She desired him.

Breathe.

Once [...] [beau]tiful, wide m[...] [...] mascu[...]

As if to [...]

Dear Reader,

With each story in The Meadows Family series, I fall in love with this family all over again. It's Fiona's turn to decide what is important in her life. I hope you enjoy this romantic journey that strums on the heartstrings and invites you to fall for this winning couple.

At the time of writing this, the announcement of David Bowie's death had hit the airwaves. A true pioneer and participant of life and music was gone. But one of the most memorable parts of his life was his love for Iman and the beautiful courtship of his soul mate that led to their marriage.

The power of love is magical, lasting and transformative.

I hope you also feel the magic with *One to Win*.

Peace,

Michelle

One to Win

Michelle Monkou

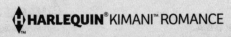

HARLEQUIN® KIMANI™ ROMANCE

Recycling programs
for this product may
not exist in your area.

ISBN-13: 978-0-373-86463-8

One to Win

Copyright © 2016 by Michelle Monkou

For questions and comments about the quality of this book please contact us at CustomerService@Harlequin.com.

Printed in U.S.A.

Michelle Monkou became a world traveler at the age of three, when she left her birthplace of London, England, and moved to Guyana, South America. She then moved to the US as a young teen. Michelle was nominated for the 2003 Emma Award for Favorite New Author, and continues to write romances with complex characters and intricate plots. Visit her website for further information at www.michellemonkou.com or contact her at michellemonkou@comcast.net.

Books by Michelle Monkou

Harlequin Kimani Romance

Sweet Surrender
Here and Now
Straight to the Heart
No One But You
Gamble on Love
Only in Paradise
Trail of Kisses
The Millionaire's Ultimate Catch
If I Had You
Racing Hearts
Passionate Game
One of a Kind
One to Love
One to Win

Visit the Author Profile page at
Harlequin.com for more titles.

To the readers who started on this journey with me since 2002, who've stuck with me with die-hard loyalty and who may just have joined the ride— thank you with all my heart.

Acknowledgments

Thanks to Carly Silver for your editorial assistance and helping make the story shine.

Chapter 1

"**B**udget cuts!" Detective Fiona Reed couldn't believe what she'd heard.

Frustration pumped anger through her veins. Her pulse pounded, accenting the soaring beat of her temper. Words bubbled up and pushed against the verbal barrier that kept her civil and respectable.

"Watch your step," Captain Baxter warned, "before you spew words that you can't pull back." His glare sparred with hers and won.

"Sir, this budget cut is…is…plain stupid. We can't get our job done with fewer hours—no overtime is nonsense. That's just dumb. Most of the victims who are listed as missing in our case files are minors. Cuts along the support staff? We need more help. It's not rocket science, what we need to solve these cases. And it's definitely not about the counselor's sound bites

harping on government waste and effective management." Her voice had escalated probably beyond the
walls of the captain's closed office. Oh, well—it wasn't
the first time that she'd delivered a vehement one-way
pitch here.

"Your area isn't the only one affected." Baxter ran
a hand over his bald head. His haggard features spoke
volumes as to his own misery as the messenger. "Every
area, department, everything, has been whittled down.
It's how things are now. We all have to deal with it.
That means you, as a team player." He stabbed at the
space between them. His thick black eyebrows drew
down over his fierce gaze.

Fiona heard the words. She listened to the message,
but none of it satisfied her. None of it deflated her irritation. The Missing Persons Unit of Essex County, New
York, needed more than the three detectives and two
clerks assigned to it. The shortage in manpower had
almost cost the lives of a set of twins who were habit-
ual runaways, but had thankfully been found. Working
around the clock wasn't the exception. Day, night and
the seconds in between, Fiona had followed every lead
to track the sisters. The fifty dollars she had to pay here
and there to get information came out of her pocket.
Whatever it took to find any of these kids, she'd try.

Bottom line, the shrinking budget mattered. With
other social services around the county getting elim-
inated or slashed, too many cases of the missing remained unsolved with stomach-churning frequency.
The deep tar pit of bureaucracy into which these people sank and disappeared from everyone's attention
twisted her gut in knots of frustration. After six years
on the job, at times it felt like an insurmountable climb

to have successful endings to the cases. If she had her wish, she'd do anything she could to double the funds to run this unit.

Fiona studied her boss's face, trying to read, trying to test, trying to gauge her footing. Where did his loyalties lie?

"Are you fighting to keep the funding?" Fiona took the plunge into volatile depths.

"Detective, watch your step." Baxter spoke softly, but his displeasure radiated like an overheated sunlamp. His neck and shoulders were rigid with his annoyance.

"We need the money." She pounded her fist into her open hand. "What we do is worth fighting for."

The captain tossed aside his pen, poised over the paperwork on the desk, and shot up with such force that his chair hit the credenza behind him. His body rose to its full towering height. His shoulders squared and his chest puffed up with his indignation. Dark brown eyes pinned her in place. Baxter clenched his hands and leaned on the desk. His breathing was heavy, nostrils flaring, as he angled into her space.

They faced off across the desk. Seconds felt like minutes. His eyes narrowed into a squint. No doubt she was in deep trouble. Not a particularly unique event in the life of her career. A stubborn streak in her refused to back down, even as the warnings flashed through her consciousness like a gaudily lit sign. She held her ground, despite a slight tremor in her knees that threatened to take over her entire body.

"You're overdue for your vacation. Take it, effective immediately," Baxter delivered with his quiet anger.

Fiona flinched from the swift punishment. "Sir, I've

got a crazy caseload on my desk. You need everyone here." Obviously, it was too late to retract or soften her belligerence.

"This isn't up for negotiation. Boggs and Fogarty will divvy up your files. You need to walk away and get your mind back in the game."

"Sir..." She was used to arguing with her captain. Those clashes might have ended in threats, scoldings, but never this...banishment.

"A vacation or a suspension. And don't try my patience. I understand that I didn't exactly come onto the scene in the best of circumstances after Captain Doyle suffered a massive heart attack. You didn't get the promotion that you wanted. And the media hasn't been supportive of the strides made by this unit. The last thing needed around here is this implosion." He folded his arms. "Now, I agree with everyone that you are a damn good detective. You've deserved every commendation. However, lately, you've been..."

"Doing my job." Fiona wasn't going down without a fight.

"Intense. Belligerent. Insubordinate. I know about your off-the-record tirade with Counselor Jenkins."

Each criticism was shot at her ego like a well-aimed dart.

"So take two weeks. Get your head together and rejoin the team."

"I don't—"

The captain held up his finger. The gesture was a distant reminder of her days in school when the teacher reprimanded her for talking out of turn.

"Yes, sir." Fiona clenched her jaw. Logic pried its way in, past the hot rush of her impatience.

"Effective immediately. Please close the door on your way out." Every syllable Baxter uttered had its own beat.

With no other choice, Fiona walked toward the door, turned the knob and opened it. Taking a deep breath and exhaling to put on a stoic face, she stepped into the hallway. But then her hand shook and she opened and closed it to steady her nerves before pulling the door shut. Then with her chin up, she returned to her cubicle.

The walk of shame was self-made. She couldn't blame a drink, a drug or lack of sleep for her brash behavior. Her colleagues avoided eye contact with her. Some even slowed and seemingly pressed their bodies against the wall as if she were contagious.

Inciting the captain's ire was a stupid career move. Instead of focusing her anger on the annoying obstacles outside of the unit, she had thrown her net wide enough to show her disrespect to the captain. She had overstepped, to put it mildly.

Acknowledging her rash behavior now didn't change her current status.

Back at her desk, she flipped open the twins' file. It could now be moved from active to closed. That should have had her doing backflips in celebration. Maybe when the turbulent emotions flagged, the brighter side of things would emerge. All she could see at this point were the photos, testimony and visual evidence of sad lives and raging emotions.

She pinched the bridge of her nose right between her eyes to inflict her own punishment. Her boss was correct. She had to deal with anger and disappointment more appropriately. Otherwise, the negative emotions would consume her, gnawing on her soul until only bitterness overtook contentment. The job and its sidecar BS got to her and screwed up her judgment.

"Hey, *chica*, you're good?" Her coworker, Detective Jacinda Mehta, asked in a husky whisper.

"Yeah." Fiona took a deep breath, doing her best to shake off the sucky vibes of failure.

"You were in there for a quite a bit." Jacinda rested her chin on the cubicle wall. "I'm making sure you still have your head."

Fiona coaxed a smile out of herself. "Still got it." She pointed upward to said body part. "Barely."

"I tried to talk you out of it." Jacinda shook her head, as she entered the cubicle. "But you were hell-bent on taking on 'the man.'" She provided air quotes that just emphasized to Fiona how harebrained and impulsive her actions had been. "So, did you get away with it? I had to head down to the evidence locker."

Fiona knew Jacinda might be worried about her, but her coworker also was ready to share a laugh at her streaks of stubbornness. "I said what I had to say."

"Fist bump, *chica*." Jacinda extended her hand.

Fiona complied. "And...I'll be taking a two-week vacation."

"Hot damn. You got a double win—telling off the boss *and* heading to the beach."

"Who said anything about the beach?" Fiona shook her head at Jacinda's excitement.

"That's where I'd go."

Fiona shrugged. The response seemed appropriate, given she hadn't weighed her options. It had been a while since she took time off. Real time off that lasted for more than a long weekend. The sun hadn't warmed her body in a while. And as for walking barefoot in the sand, that hadn't happened in a couple years. The idea of kicking back felt strange and wrong to entertain when she had a caseload the height of a Midtown Manhattan skyscraper. But the matter was no longer hers to consider.

"Look, do I need to give you a list of destinations to visit?"

Fiona shook her head. Any suggestions courtesy of Jacinda might land her at an expensive resort halfway around the world. Her colleague loved to cherry-pick interesting male partners on her various trips.

For her part, Fiona preferred a good book and a glass of wine—alone. She was over the manhunt for a good while. Her recently ended relationship with a man who was oversexed, uncommunicative *and* bad at kissing helped to instill her current priority system.

Desperate wasn't her middle name.

Later that day, Fiona gathered at her cousin's house in Midway, New York, where her other cousins waited. Belinda's place was often their mutually agreed setting to catch up. After her latest drama, the others wanted a blow-by-blow account of her issues on the job.

"Wow. What a story. You are lucky that your boss didn't write you up." Her cousin Dana interrupted for the umpteenth time, no longer trying to hold in her amusement.

"Humph!" Fiona hadn't stopped fuming, although she had to admit that her punishment could have been worse.

"Now you can go with us to the Hamptons." Belinda emerged from the house and stepped onto the deck.

One hand balanced the drinks and the other held a plate with slices of her homemade peach-almond cake.

"Grace doesn't know my situation changed." Fiona accepted the proffered iced tea and helped by taking the plate of sliced cakes and setting it on her lap.

"No, you don't." Dana promptly removed the plate and placed it on the small table centered in front of the three women. "Belinda, you always have the best snacks for our gab sessions."

"My pleasure, ladies." Belinda looked pleased at their murmurs of appreciation as they munched and washed down the treats.

The September weather still held on to the last dregs of summer's humidity. Upstate New York hadn't escaped the oppressive blanket of hot and sticky temperatures. But for Fiona, the hellish conditions felt right for sitting on the deck, soaking up the sun, pigging out on cake and drowning her sorrows in iced tea.

Belinda's home was always the cousins' fun hangout place. Although her cousin's charming boyfriend had become a familiar presence, Jesse Santiago knew when the women needed their alone time. Now that Jesse had permanently closed the door to his soccer career to run his father's construction business, he had blended into Belinda's world and shared her love for horses. Most of his free time, except for when he was with Belinda, was spent riding around the large property or performing any rehab needed on the physical structure of the equine therapy facility.

After sampling another slice of cake, Fiona pointed at Dana. "I don't hear you confirming my statement that Grace doesn't know about my situation." Fiona unfolded her legs from her seated position and sat up.

"Please tell me that you didn't throw me under the bus with our grandmother."

"Way under the bus, like six feet under." Belinda tossed back her head as she expelled a hearty laugh.

"Why should we be the only ones that have to go to the Hamptons?" Dana's mouth closed into a pout.

Belinda took up the defense against Fiona. "You know Grace feels that it is a family tradition to have one vacation together—our annual Meadows family duty."

"But it's not really a vacation. Our family under one roof is chaos. Drama with a capital *D*. That's not a vacation. Besides, let's stop pretending that we are this family dynasty, like the Kennedys or Rockefellers, operating like we are like this." Fiona held up her hands pressed together with interlocked fingers to indicate closeness.

She didn't care that the family did show up to the various gatherings. If her grandmother didn't insist on having her usual expectation heeded, the family wouldn't operate like a close-knit unit. The reason they did was clear—it wasn't because they wanted to be together.

Despite all of Grace's accomplishments, she couldn't brag about the bond between her and her three daughters. Their mothers all had a mixture of respect and awe for Grace, but all had endured her hands-on, sometimes manipulative nurturing.

Verona, Fiona's mother, who also was Grace's eldest daughter, had the most strained relationship, with no signs of improvement over the years. Whatever history had passed between her mother and Grace remained unknown, although their measured approach to each other was quite visible. Regardless of her cousins' endorsement, going to the Hamptons did not rank as one of Fiona's favorite ways to spend family time.

Dana leaned forward, resting her elbows on her knees. "What else would you be doing? You are now a benched superhero of the police department. And for the record, I plan to continue this family-vacation tradition when that time regretfully comes." Her dark brown eyes reflected sincerity.

"Okay, now that you've taken over from Grace to be the CEO of the family media conglomerate, don't let it go to your head. You're supposed to be on our rebel side," Belinda reminded her.

"Yeah, well…" Dana swallowed the rest of her defense in a long drink from her glass.

"Maybe I can grovel and get my vacation postponed." Fiona's forehead was still furrowed as she resumed reclining with her legs tucked to the side. She munched on a piece of ice.

"From what you've told me, I foresee that if you step foot into that office, you'll regret it. Your boss may be new, but he seems to be as tough as a junkyard dog. So go ahead and disobey his order. I'll sit back and wait to tell you 'I told you so.'" Dana's mouth pursed full of smugness.

"You were always the mean one," Fiona accused. Defeat set in, ratcheting up her grumpiness.

"That's why she's running the Meadows empire. Someone's got to walk in Grace's queenly footsteps." Belinda jabbed her thumb in the air toward their youngest cousin.

"Stop calling Meadows Media an empire. And

I'm not mean. I'm doling out the appropriate advice, that's all."

Fiona ignored the bickering and drained her glass to chew on more ice. "Looks like I'm going to the Hamptons." Something she'd suspected she'd get roped into when the invitation had come from Grace two months ago.

Grace had a reputation for approaching each granddaughter with an invitation to join Meadows Media. Her invitation was predictable and always managed to tweak a bit of guilt from the ones who didn't join the company after graduating from college.

"Let's move this inside now. I'm melting and I just got my hair done. My honey and I are going on a date tonight." Belinda stood and brushed off the crumbs.

"I don't want to hear about any lovey-dovey stuff." Fiona hurried ahead of Dana into the cool indoors. "I seem to attract men who can't handle a woman working a demanding job or men who need to be put on a pedestal to be worshipped."

"It's a bit more than that, Fiona." Belinda was busy in the kitchen, retrieving fresh glasses for the delicious fruit punch spiked with a touch of white rum. "You, my dear, are a workaholic. You thrive off of four hours of sleep. You are prone to canceling dates. And you'd rather spend your free time with us than staring deeply into a sexy, horny man's eyes."

Dana puckered her mouth and made kissing sounds.

"Well, sue me for thinking that y'all were cool with hanging out together."

"Stop whining. I'm not the one giving you a diagnosis. However, I will say that you need to take these two weeks to relax. Then you can go back and be refreshed for the never-ending wave of cases that come across your desk." Dana grabbed hold of Fiona's shoulders and massaged them.

"Maybe I should change what I'm doing." Fiona wanted to test the waters with her cousins about the latest thoughts burdening her.

"What?" Belinda walked out with the second round of drinks and handed one to each. "Okay, you really need to come to the Hamptons. We should talk about all this in a different setting. You sound like you need a life intervention when absolutely nothing is wrong with you."

"Oh, right, like I really need to figure out my future under Grace's nose. If I recall, she has been all over both of you about holding down the family business. You, Dana, stepped up, but it was a no-brainer because you have the passion and business brains to run Meadows Media. And you, Belinda, you stood your ground to build your equine therapy center from the ground up. Now that leaves me to hold my stance with her or surrender and take the offer to be the head of Meadows security." Fiona batted her eyelashes at Dana. "May I be your bodyguard?"

Dana waved off her silliness.

"Oh, this is going to be fun." Belinda was too cheerful for Fiona's liking. "Consider the exercise of finding your path a rite of passage. And you get to go through it at a prime beachfront location."

Although Belinda's buildup sounded good, from Fiona's headspace, the "rite of passage" didn't fill her with a cheery disposition. She really was questioning her future and to be faced with Grace's intense focus on the family's legacy and the cousins' roles in continuing the decades of success made her stomach flip and flop and tie itself into knots.

"Would it help if I said that Leo Starks will be there?" Dana's voice dropped low and seductive.

"Leo? The same Leo Starks?" Fiona kept her gaze on the golden liquid in her glass, a mix of naturally sweet tropical fruits. She couldn't blame the splash of alcohol for the instant flush to her cheeks. "Why will he be there?"

Dana's expression just about glowed over the news. Her animated hand gestures added emphasis. "Word is that he's there at Grace's invitation. She was always impressed with him, from his days as a legal intern several years ago at Meadows to landing a job at Grayson, Buckley and Tynesdale after he earned his law degree. No real information about the reason for his presence, though. And Grace is not telling. But that will make it more fun for you to sniff out why your onetime Brazilian Sweet Lips is coming to the Hamptons."

"Don't call him that." Fiona had to agree that the moniker was 100 percent accurate, but she wasn't sure if said lips were still one of Leo's most attractive points. "So Starks will be there? For the entire stay?" Her cheeks remained warm. The sensation spread over her entire face and down her neck, as if she sat too close to a roaring fireplace.

Memories of Leo Starks didn't float away into the black hole of forgotten experiences. Falling in love had the power to keep its hook in for the long haul. Though she'd allowed doubt to creep in like wild weeds and fracture what they had between them, she couldn't close the door completely on their special time.

Dana shrugged her slender shoulders. "I don't know

if he'll be there for the entire month. I can only stick around for the first week."

Belinda raised her hands. "I'm there for two, but Jesse will come back to the center after one week. And, yes, I'm making him attend. He might as well see us in all our glory if he's going to be a permanent part of this family."

"Oh my gosh, did he propose?" Dana asked, while Fiona screamed with joy.

"No. Don't rush us. But we are truly committed to each other. I haven't been this happy in a long time." Belinda's voice dipped with a tender note.

The two cousins had stopped their excited outbursts, but they grinned at Belinda's declaration.

"I'll stay as long as you all are there." Fiona loved seeing her cousins immersed in their loving relationships with the special men in their lives.

Love had played the chasing game with all of them, but now her cousins had nabbed their perfect soul mates. She tried not to wonder when she'd get so lucky. Or maybe the reality was *if* she would get so lucky. The thought of falling in love without a safety net, revealing the inner private side of her life, caused a queasy, weak-kneed reaction in Fiona. Not her thing. She'd rather convince herself that the tender side of life, where soulful sighs and sensuous cravings resided, wasn't a high priority.

"I suspect that you'll stay as long as Leo is there," Dana teased in a singsong voice.

"He means nothing to me."

"Don't toss that out so fast. You're not fooling us. I know you sampled those gorgeous lips when he was an intern at Meadows." Belinda took up the baton of teasing and echoed Dana with a series of exaggerated kissing sounds.

"Who's got gorgeous lips?" A familiar deep male voice interrupted the noisy exchange among the cousins.

Silence. Then the women erupted into fits of giggles.

"You, baby." Belinda opened her arms in invitation to Jesse. Without hesitation, he stepped into her embrace, where she locked him to her chest. No complaints came from him as Belinda planted a wet, sloppy kiss before releasing her man.

Fiona and Dana groaned and made a show of shielding their eyes.

"On that note, Dana, let's go. Take me home. I think the lovebirds are not going to wait for us to leave before the scene turns into Mature Audiences Only. And I'm too young to see any of this." Fiona grabbed her cousin's arm for their quick goodbye. "Besides, I'm sure your love muffin is also home waiting for you."

"Now you sound like you're hatin'. But yeah, Kent is home. Tomorrow he's heading back to England to be a coach for the executive staff of an airline. Fingers crossed that he'll be back in time to spend a few days at the Hamptons. We both need the time off."

Fiona nodded. How would she survive being surrounded by couples madly in love?

As they walked to Dana's car, her cousin playfully bumped Fiona's shoulder. "Thinking about the owner of those wicked cheekbones and that chiseled jawline? I remember when those females at Meadows Media were salivating every time he arrived. Emails would whip through the office with the announcement. Yet you were the only lucky one from the company to road test those lips. Maybe more than that?" Dana aimed the car remote at her Audi and popped open the locks. She leaned against the car and continued, "And that's my dose of encouragement for you to look forward to the Hamptons. In two days, your secret nighttime thoughts and the sexy reality can become one."

"And that's what I'm afraid of," Fiona mumbled as Dana got into the car.

"I'm rooting for you."

She took a moment longer than Dana to get in the car. Her imagination wasn't waiting for the darkness of her bedroom to go to work. If the embarrassing memories of those hot kisses kept up, tonight she'd suffer a sleepless night, tossing and turning in her bed from reawakened delicious torment.

On the ride home, she was mostly silent. Along with recalling the unusual passionate response to Leo's touch, she also couldn't ignore the thought that she'd ultimately rejected him three years ago. Back then, her fear of love and all its side effects was more potent and undisciplined. Now the fear had become ingrained like a habit that could be relied upon in other relationships, but one that provided zero comfort to her soul. A year and a few days with Leo as a friend and lover had changed her life, her outlook and what she desired in her heart. She'd never moved on, knowing that she'd made a huge mistake. All she'd wanted was to let him go so he could fulfill his dreams of being a top-notch lawyer without the added stress of an unlikely romance. All around her, women—her mother, aunts, even grandmother—had life stories where career and romance were two colliding forces that demanded their time and energy. Their men seemed the exception to the rule of finding that precious balance, without setting conditions on their partners. Fiona didn't ever want to force sacrifices or obligations on anyone. In an impulsive move, she'd taken a stance and lived to regret it.

In two days there would be a chance for a do-over or maybe a continuation of this unresolved episode between them. The possibility of an amended ending, however, didn't hold any promise of a change of heart. There still would be no commitment. She didn't believe in surrendering every part of her soul into the heady mix of deep emotions; love would eventually get ripped apart, either because a couple grew distant and fell out of love or because the randomness of life had a way of snatching someone away. Her job taught her that one, while her childhood with an emotionally distant mother and emotionally constrained father left her unsure of what was best when it came to opening up and being vulnerable and in love.

On the other hand, Leo had been so hurt by her rejection that he'd probably moved on to someone who appreciated him. Someone who didn't live life with that undercurrent of fear guiding important decisions.

By the time Fiona climbed into bed for the night, she toyed with the thin sliver of a chance that she would have a change of heart. Dare she entertain the possibility? Was she up for a second attempt with Leo Starks? She hugged her pillow and closed her eyes. His face filled her memory. A small smile curved her lips. She could hear the unique cadence of his voice in her head. And he was the best kisser…ever.

A vacation at the Hamptons suddenly had great appeal.

What to do when Grace Meadows sent an invitation that was really a command? Leo knew his response would be clear in two days when he arrived at the family's eleven-acre vacation estate in the Hamptons.

"Leo Starks, you *are* the man." His coworker collapsed into the nearest chair in his office.

Leo ignored Eric, although he knew that wouldn't stop the envious jabs thinly disguised as ribbing. Working on anything related to the Meadows Media business was not just a perk but a guaranteed career boost at Grayson, Buckley and Tynesdale.

Although Grace Meadows was no longer leading Meadows Media, she had a sizable net worth that required her to have the best legal counsel. His firm had served both the personal and public sides of the Meadows family for two decades. Now the next generation of lawyers was being groomed to smooth the transition as staff retired. To be selected for that esteemed position took hard work and long hours, the savvy to navigate the sharklike office politics, and, of a more personal nature, a passion for looking out for the rights of his clients.

All of that didn't matter if Grace was unhappy with any part of their service. Heaven help the person who ticked off the indomitable woman with error or incompetence. That lawyer might as well voluntarily banish himself to the darkest, coldest and most wretched place in the world.

"Not too many of us mortals have visited the palatial digs in Water Mill. I could put four of my condos in that house and still have room."

"It's not a vacation, Eric. And imagine working under Grace's scrutiny for an unknown number of days." Leo tried to dim his excitement. Plus there was the potential to see Fiona. As far as he knew, the entire Meadows family was expected to show up. The grain of hope for a meet-up with his ex had steadily expanded to the point where his gut now reacted under the flurry of what-if scenarios.

"Come on—cough up the details. What are you working on with Meadows? Another company in the mix? Will she need more lawyers working on a project?" Eric fired his questions at Leo without a breath between each piercing inquiry. His colleague's easy smile faded into a mask of intensity.

"Aren't you on the Van Buren files? That's a hot new opportunity." Leo did his best to push Eric back into his own lane. His connection to the Meadows family, whether because of his work or because of his romantic past with one of the granddaughters, wasn't going to be part of any discussion with his colleague.

"Yeah, they've come into new money." Eric shrugged, clearly unimpressed by the recently acquired wealth.

"Still, it pays the bills. Yours."

"Yeah. But I'm going for the big guns." Eric scooted his chair closer to Leo's desk. "So, like I said, if they need additional lawyers, don't forget to play nice and share the toys." His gleaming white teeth were bared in a fake grin.

"I'll keep that in mind." Leo pushed back his chair

and stood. This conversation was over. He deliberately used all of his six-foot-five-inch frame to dominate his annoying colleague. "It's time for me to get out of here."

"Okay." Eric rose out of the chair and took a step in retreat. "Coming with the guys to the usual hangout?"

Leo shook his head. "I have to pack. Enjoy a drink on me."

"Cool. And I'll text you about what hot babes I landed for the weekend. You know they are suckers for us lawyers." He slid his hand along the side of his head. His sleek black hair was always in place, trimmed, a ready magnet for the women.

Leo accepted that he was a nerd. Nothing about his looks stirred a stampede of women toward him. According to his male colleagues, he needed to loosen up and stop scowling. The women who showered him with their suggestions for improvement shared the belief that his eyes were too serious and intense for someone his age. His short last relationship ended with her saying that he was too young to act so old. Apparently, his speedy retreat from her surprise weekend trip to a nudist camp for swingers in Oregon did them in. Some things, he couldn't unsee.

"Here's my last bit of advice. Don't get in the tabloids with the Meadows granddaughters. Now, that would be a threesome to end all threesomes." Eric grinned and slipped out of Leo's office whistling a nameless tune.

"What an idiot," Leo remarked in the empty office. He got his briefcase and suit jacket and headed out of the building.

The oppressive heat walloped his face with its humidity. He hurried to his car, grateful to set the air vents on a cold maximum blast. The car's interior took its time cooling while he sat with his hands clenching and unclenching around the steering wheel. His thoughts wouldn't let up on the barrage. What would happen when he crossed paths with Fiona Reed?

Their mismatched hookup had been kept a secret from most. The reactions and snide comments had hit their mark: a young lawyer dating an older woman had raised a few eyebrows, caused a few jokes at his expense. An intern dating his employer's eldest granddaughter had prompted whispered warnings to be careful because it was career suicide. A man who'd fallen hopelessly and secretly in love with this woman. A woman who refused to see him as more than a casual boyfriend. A painful memory that he carried with him, and a heart that had suffered the way she'd trampled over it during her departure from his life.

Leo headed for home. He had a lot to do before he got on the road. Fate had a way of paving the path with opportunities. But opportunities weren't always a good thing; they were merely a chance to make a decision. A part of him, where feelings, emotions and possibilities resided, craved the idea of a second chance.

His feelings, however, were hung up on his first fall into real love. The tumble was hard and the wounds ran deep. Frustration that he'd let go so easily drew bitterness. And disappointment certainly had a way of following him through his life. After his heart was broken by Fiona, he'd understood the lesson—to avoid any more strong emotional entanglements. But his mind wouldn't let go and he hated to admit that his heart hadn't moved on.

He turned into his driveway, activated the garage door to open and eased his car into the space. To his right was a spot for another car. His empty house had enough rooms for a large family and pets. Everything was in place, except the woman who'd torn his heart in two. He'd lived a rough and poor life as a child where forgiveness was a sign of weakness and trust was not to be given so easily. His lessons had been learned the hard way. And no matter how his defenses could crumble at the sight of Fiona, his head was in charge for this go-round.

Pride, resolve and the bitter taste of rejection had more power than the desire to cave in and be grateful that he'd be sharing the same space with her. He shook his head in response to his weakening resolve. There would be no second chances.

Chapter 2

Fiona didn't wait until Sunday to drive to the Hamptons. Her nerves wouldn't allow her to reach a relaxed state to wait out the weekend. By Saturday afternoon, she was in her car heading south on the highway. The long drive gave enough time for her to mentally prepare for the arduous tasks of dealing with her grandmother, enjoying a vacation forced by her boss and holding field advantage for Leo's arrival. The last item held the most importance.

To be held in those arms, tight against his chest, close enough to hear his heart beat its deep, pulsing rhythm—she sighed over her fantasy. Anticipation grew as she gazed at the mileage signs toward New York City that steadily decreased as she neared her destination. Her foot pushed on the gas pedal in a coordinated effort with her desire to hasten her arrival.

By nightfall she'd reached the family estate. It felt good to have her feet on solid ground.

"Good evening, Miss Fiona. Welcome back. Hope you had a good drive."

Fiona nodded and entered the house. "Thank you, Mrs. Finch. The drive had some teeth this time. Heavy traffic. Roadwork." Fiona torqued her body to work out the kinks along her back and hips. Seven hours and then some, driving over and through the mountains with tractor trailers for company, did challenge her reflexes. She looked forward to a long soak in the pool-sized bathtub in her room to find her Zen.

"Your room is ready. Denton will park the car and take up your luggage. Don't worry about a thing. Will you be dining in your room?"

Fiona nodded with an apologetic scrunch of her nose. "I hate to be a pain."

"Grilled cheese with bacon. Tall glass of milk. Two chocolate chip cookies." Mrs. Finch's rosy cheeks bunched with the wide smile.

"You know me so well." Fiona hugged the house manager, whom she'd known since she was ten years old. "Anyone else crashed early?"

"Mrs. Grace and Mr. Henry are here. They arrived on Thursday. After a full day in the vegetable garden today, they both headed up early."

Despite the brilliantly lit entry room, the sitting rooms on either side of the area were dim. A comfortable silence hung over the house. Well, all of that would change when her cousins invaded the castle walls.

"And my parents?" Fiona looked toward the staircase that stood as the prominent fixture in the middle of the black-and-white-marbled entryway.

"They haven't arrived. But their room is ready for whenever they do."

Fiona didn't expect her mother to show up tomorrow. If Fiona felt reluctance to come to the vacation home, her mother experienced dread, an emotion that she barely concealed, and the source was a fairly new annoying mystery. If Grace was the cause, there was no evidence to prove the case. When Fiona asked her mother if she was okay or invited her to share why she was troubled, she was usually pointedly ignored. Yet Fiona couldn't pretend that she didn't care if her mom showed up. They were all in this family reunion, for better or worse.

"You look like you need a good night's rest. Go on to the room and I'll have your dinner sent up."

"Thanks, Mrs. Finch. Can't wait for those cookies." Fiona left the car keys with her to pass on to Denton to park the car. Then she ran up the grand staircase that curved off to the left and right. Its polished walnut banister accented the crisp white stairs. Her hand glided along the wood with appreciation for the perfect slide it had made back in the day for her and her cousins. The prohibited activity was also the reason for her many time-outs when she was caught by Mrs. Finch or, worse, by her grandmother. She smiled at the memories.

Fiona opened the bedroom and entered her personal space. All three cousins would stay on the same floor in side-by-side rooms. The aunts and uncles and her parents would stay in the other wing on the same level. But she wondered where Leo would lay his head. How hospitable was Grace feeling? The house was large enough for him to stay in one of the many guest rooms, but there was also the cottage off to the side of the property that could be used.

A knock on the door interrupted her reacquaintance with the room.

"Come in."

A maid entered with the tray. "Hi, Miss Fiona, I'm Shawna. I'm new here."

"Hi, nice to meet you. I'll take the tray." She crossed the room and retrieved the platter with all the tasty indulgences that Mrs. Finch had promised. She put it down on her bed.

As soon as the maid left, Fiona stripped off her clothes, grabbed the tray and headed for the bathroom. In no time, Fiona prepared her bath. The water steamed the mirrors and the suds were pleasantly thick, filling the room with a wonderful vanilla scent. After a bit of maneuvering, she had the tray set on a small table next to the tub.

Fiona sank down into the tub until the water covered her breasts. Her sigh was loud and full of her satisfaction. She reached for the sandwich first and bit into the warm bread and welcomed the gooey cheese. No doubt she'd be spoiled by Mrs. Finch's staff before her two weeks ended.

Her phone rang. She gingerly pushed the talk button with her pinkie finger.

"Fiona? Where are you?" Dana's question had a shrill edge.

"In my favorite bathtub. Eating my favorite sandwich—"

"I can't believe you headed out early. And didn't tell us. You're wrong for that." Dana carried on with her complaints.

"It's not as if we were riding together."

"Yeah, but you're in that fab house. And I'm eating a Chinese dinner by myself. I miss Kent."

Fiona took another bite of her sandwich. "Stop whining. Just come out early in the morning."

Dana mocked her by echoing her statement.

"Uncalled for. And I'm about to hang up." Fiona eyed the other half of her sandwich, which she wanted to consume in peace.

"Wait. I've got some details about your guy."

"Not my guy."

"Then you don't need to know. Never mind."

Dana's teasing irritated Fiona's resolve to maintain indifference under her cousins' scrutiny.

"What's going on?" Fiona gritted her teeth over Dana's laughter.

"The reason for him being at the Hamptons is definitely a big secret."

"You are really messing with my vibe." Fiona put down the sandwich that she'd just picked up and waited for her annoying cousin to cough up information. "So Grace told you why Leo will be there?"

"I did ask and was told that it didn't concern me. When it was the appropriate time, she would tell me. Then I got the dial tone."

Fiona chuckled. "I give you points for going straight to Grace. But that's not really clarifying anything."

"I didn't say that I was done. I asked Grandpa Henry."

"So now you're ready to get him kicked to the couch." Fiona reached for a cookie instead. This conversation was getting better.

Dana laughed. "Grandpa knows how to handle his wife. Anyway, he said that Grace was meddling in stuff that she shouldn't be. He also said that we'd need to remember that we are a family."

"That sounds ominous."

"He looked worried, but I'd say that he was more… um…introspective, and a bit sad."

Fiona didn't like secrets. The burden to hold them close could be unbearable. And her grandmother was the perfect type to have a bank vault of secrets. The Meadows matriarch was a planner and oftentimes a manipulator, but she was also a woman who'd had to work her way up in a man's world. No doubt Grace had probably seen and done her share of the unmentionable.

"And what has that got to do with Leo?" Fiona didn't bother to shade her curiosity with subtlety.

"Is he good with secrets?"

Fiona didn't have to ponder the question. She had firsthand knowledge of their secret relationship and how Leo had done everything to keep it under wraps. He was always so concerned about his career and doing something to mess with his plans to fast-track the career ladder. "Good luck with trying to find out anything from Leo."

"That's why you're the one to pry it from him. This is important." Dana would not let her interrupt. "I'm not doubting Grandpa Henry's feelings. Whatever is going on sounds as if it involves the family."

Fiona felt a momentary pulse of panic. "I don't need you giving me a job while I'm here. I'll probably barely see Leo. And we don't know when he'll arrive."

"Grandpa Henry clamped his mouth shut when I pushed about Leo. Can't tell if he likes the man."

"What's there not to like?" Fiona blurted with a heavy dose of defensiveness.

"I don't know, Fiona—tell me. You walked away from him."

"My bathwater is cold. Time for me to get ready for my comfy bed. Enjoy the drive." Retreat was a wiser choice.

Dana sucked in a breath. "Sorry. Didn't mean to pinch your nerve. See you tomorrow, cousin."

"Drive safely." Fiona hung up.

Her mood, like her once-heated water, had cooled, turning stormy and restless with what was to come. Instead of wondering how her first meeting with Leo would turn out, now she was wondering more about why he had been invited to the family retreat. If Grandpa Henry was troubled, then the problem had to be a doozy.

"Leo Starks, what have you gotten yourself into with the Meadows family?"

After dressing for bed, Fiona parted the thick drapes at the window with her hand and peered out into the inky darkness that blanketed the wide expanse of land. The house sat recessed from the main road with its backside close to the bay. Tomorrow she'd catch up with her grandmother. Then she could take a quick walk around to see what had changed or been updated. But she hoped that here, at her perch, she'd have the ideal view to see everyone pull up to the front door. Staking her position at this perfect lookout gave her a smidgen of confidence for the eventual meeting between her and Leo.

* * *

"Well, damn, and well, damn." Leo slowed to a stop and shifted the gear to Park.

He needed a moment to take in the sight in front of him. Not only was the sunrise a vivid fusion of color and brilliance, but its position just over the rooftop created a postcard effect. The house was something out of a movie. If he didn't think Eric would lose his mind and do something idiotic, he'd take a photo with his cell phone and send the image to his coworker for the sheer pleasure of witnessing his ugly fall into deeper envy.

Leo's own admiration had nothing to do with jealousy. The architecture soaked up his appreciation, thanks to a youthful pastime of studying the great builders in history. Though this impressive home had all the modern amenities and an expansive structure, he recognized the basic design from the 1920s, when industrialists flaunted their wealth from the blossoming American industrial economy with opulent family homes.

The Colonial Revival was typical of this area. Despite the contemporary touches, the British Georgian influence made its bold mark on the house with the symmetrical shuttered windows placed on either side of the door. Although the land was relatively flat, the house, with its two floors and broad, gabled roof, stood on a raised dune. Parked at the curve of the mile-long driveway, Leo understood why the original owner had chosen this parcel of land to show off this jewel. Every morning, the residents probably enjoyed the pleasure of seeing the sun's rise with a fiery dawn kiss on the landscape. He looked forward to sharing in the experience.

After a few more seconds of staring at the view, Leo

shifted the car into Drive and steered toward the most important assignment of his career. As he approached, other cars parked in front of the house came into sight. He pulled up behind the last one, stopped the engine and got out. His gaze took in the surrounding area and the close-up version of the estate.

"You must be Leo Starks."

Leo nodded to the woman who emerged from the car in front of his. He waited for her to reveal her identity.

"Belinda." She stepped away from her car with her outstretched hand. The warm smile eased his nerves. "I'm one of the granddaughters. And that's Dana."

He gave Dana a wave in answer to hers. This was cousin number two, the CEO. He recognized her from afar. So where was the third cousin? Where was Fiona?

"Come, let's go in." Belinda had her arm hooked in Dana's as they marched their way to the open door.

"And I'm Jesse." A man who was left behind by the women stepped up to shake Leo's hand. "You'll get used to being ignored by them."

An older woman stood in the front doorway. "Please leave your luggage inside, near the door. And come in, come in, all of you."

Leo followed the woman's orders. She reminded him of his visa sponsor, Freida Elderhaus, the woman who was like a second mother to him.

After all the introductions, he stayed put, not sure what his next order of business would be.

"We're heading up to Fiona's. I know she's up. I saw her looking out at us from her bedroom window." Belinda was halfway up the stairs when she turned and looked directly at Leo. "I wonder who she was waiting to see."

"Couldn't be us," Dana offered.

Leo cleared his throat. He wasn't sure, but it felt like the cousins had marked him to be teased and taunted about Fiona. That was not what he wanted with Grace somewhere in the vicinity.

"Jesse, you are upstairs to the right. You're in the last room at the end of the hall." Mrs. Finch was clearly in charge of the operations. "And Mr. Starks—"

"Please, call me Leo."

She nodded. "Leo, you will be staying upstairs on the left."

"Oh no, he's with the adults," Belinda yelled down from where she hung over the rail.

"Now, that should make things interesting." Dana cocked an eyebrow as she needled him with her remark, but it was more about the pointed tone. "Fiona, aren't you going to come out here and greet your cousins?"

Mrs. Finch tsked and walked away shaking her head. "This house is about to get rowdy, Leo."

Jesse had long since gone, leaving Leo on his slow walk up the stairs.

A door opened behind him from the second floor. He continued up the stairs, knowing that when he rounded the curve of the staircase, he'd see who had emerged.

"Leo, meet our cousin Fiona." Belinda chuckled.

"But I think you know each other." Dana's face was turned toward Fiona.

And so was his.

Fiona, *his* Fiona, stood outside what he presumed

was her bedroom. He immediately looked into those big brown eyes assessing him. He returned the favor, checking out and appreciating her beauty. Thick black hair framed her face and hung down past her slender shoulders. Her brown skin glowed under the natural lighting. His fingers itched to reacquaint themselves with its smooth softness.

He had to concentrate to quell the desire to run up the stairs and nervously wait for the okay to embrace her. Instead he gripped the rail and concentrated on each measured step. His gaze stayed put on her face, gauging her stoic expression for any clue to her thoughts.

Did her excitement match his?

Did her pulse pound in anticipation of the first moment that they would have to talk to each other?

Did she suffer from the same anxious twitches in the stomach, rapid breathing and sudden dryness of the mouth?

His foot took the last step onto the second floor. Time to act unfazed. He took a deep breath and exhaled. "Hi, Fiona."

She nodded, curt and unsmiling. Her lips pressed tight with no twitch of a smile to acknowledge him.

"We'll be off so you can catch up." Again Belinda took off with her cousin, arm in arm, heading down the hall away from where he and Fiona stood like statues.

The woman, although standing still watching him, was no statue. Three years might not be a significant length of time relative to a decade or a century. But face-to-face with her beauty—natural and exquisite—those thousand-plus days stretched out like eternity. His gaze covered her entire body, and he noted that not much had changed. Average height, hair styled into gentle curls that fell just past her shoulders. Slender frame. More on the thin side, which he knew was due to her forgetfulness about eating rather than vanity. In her dress, arms bare, legs were free to be admired. He drank in the sight of her smooth skin.

He tucked his hands in his pockets to mask the nervousness, their need to trace the lines of her limbs, to brush his fingers along the delicious brown palette of her skin.

"Good to see you," she said, although her expression didn't quite match the greeting.

"You, too," he replied. Her physical beauty hadn't changed, but there was something different about her. A fleeting nuance to her, or around her, that he couldn't quite pin down. Something that was more on the inside than the outside.

"I was surprised to hear that you were coming here. Work or pleasure?"

"Work." He didn't mean to bark. "I'm working on…a project."

She walked toward him and it took everything in him to stay his ground. The soft scent of her perfume teased him, letting him know that she might be near at hand but was completely untouchable.

"And what is that project? What exactly is here that requires your service while we're on vacation?" Her eyes issued a challenge.

"It's of a personal nature. With your grandmother."

She cocked her head to the side. Her steady eye contact pierced at his defenses. "This mysterious project must be urgent."

He shrugged. "That, I don't know."

"I guess you'll find out soon." She turned to walk away but then stopped. "How long are you staying?"

"As long as your grandmother needs me to be here."

"That must be an awful lot of underwear to pack." She gave him a smile through the teasing, the first one she'd offered since seeing him.

Leo grasped at it, like a thirsty man at a well. He grinned back and nodded. "Pretty much. I'm all set."

"That's nice to know, Mr. Starks." The sharp, no-nonsense comment from a familiar older voice had the effect of a flash freeze over him and Fiona.

Grace Meadows walked into view. He'd seen her only in suits and always dressed quite professionally. Today her appearance had switched from the severe conservative businesswoman to a softer, relaxed image.

"Mr. Starks, you're staring. Fiona, you're no better. Don't you have something to get into with your cousins?" Grace motioned for her granddaughter to get moving.

Leo couldn't help staring, but his focus wasn't due to what Grace had said. The visual effect of the older and younger women standing close together was remarkable. Of course, they were related, but their striking similarities in poise and beauty hadn't really hit him until now, in this awkwardly growing moment.

Before he could explain, Fiona flew from the scene, stealing glances over her shoulder. Meanwhile, he saw her future mature elegance within the matriarch of the family, who stood next to him with a stern look on her face.

Grace cleared her throat. "Will you need to rest up?"

"Not necessary at all."

"Good. Meet me downstairs in my office and we'll get started. We can talk over coffee."

Leo didn't move until Grace had walked down to the first floor. Then he took a deep breath and gazed down the empty hallway where Fiona had disappeared. She'd have to wait.

He didn't need any further reminders from Grace that this wasn't a vacation. Instead of heading down the opposite hallway to his room, he went back downstairs and retrieved his briefcase from Denton, who was on his way up with the luggage.

"In here, Mr. Starks."

"Mrs. Meadows, we've worked together. I'd feel a lot more comfortable if you'd call me Leo." He paused. "And I will call you Grace."

She nodded. "Perfect tone to set. Leo. Please help yourself to breakfast. Then let's get to work."

Leo nodded and aimed for the coffee. He didn't have much of an appetite and probably wouldn't until he found out the real reason why he was there.

"I want my will amended."

He nodded, acknowledging the assignment to work on the will that he'd been given by the senior partner. The task would require more than his eyes and attention, but she'd insisted that he should be the only one to work on it. Although her compliments boosted his ego, her sole choice of him for this job was odd.

"Before we get the will adjusted to my new specifications, I would like to move your attention to a more pressing matter."

"Okay." Leo set down the coffee cup. The mysterious tone added another layer to the tension that had his gut doing a dance, waiting for Grace's full explanation.

"It's a delicate matter…"

"May I remind you that I am ethical?"

"Oh, I wasn't questioning that, but I did sense that you are friends with my granddaughter." She tapped her finger against her cheek as she studied him. "You are friendly with Fiona?"

"No…yes…well, a long time ago. We parted ways." Leo hadn't stuttered like this since middle school. "Today was the first time since we'd…"

"Ah, young people these days like to tiptoe toward each other." She steepled her hands. "Well, this makes things even more delicate. You see…I am handing over the entire matter for you to handle because I'm confident that you can."

"Good to have your support. But maybe that will change once I know what it is and if I'm really capable of meeting your expectations." Leo had the feeling that whatever Grace was dancing around would not have an easy solution.

"One month ago, I learned that my daughter Verona had another child. A son." Grace clutched her napkin. "I want him found—quickly and quietly."

"Yes, ma'am." Leo needed a moment to let the news sink in. "I'm not a detective."

"I don't expect you to personally find the boy. Well, by now, he's a man. And when he is found, I want him included in my will."

"But I don't know how long this will take."

"I am sure that it won't take long. And with everyone here under the same roof, I think it is an ideal time for this matter to be resolved. I want my family, every member, to be taken care of in my will." She played with the collar of her blouse. "Would be nice to see him, don't you think so, Leo?"

"Um…yes, Grace." Leo was still stuck on the fact that there was a grandson who might not have a clue about his birth mother and family.

"Not a word of this may be discussed with any member of my family. I will share any news with my husband. But I know my granddaughters will press you for answers. And I'm certain that Fiona will be the one to attempt to draw it from you. I saw how infatuated you are with her. Likewise, she is with you." She raised her hand at his protest. "I may be old, but I'm not clueless. But please take care to keep your head."

"I'm not one to cave and lose my integrity."

"Good. For the child, my grandson, is Fiona's brother."

"Oh…I see." Hard as it would be, Leo was glad that he'd decided to keep Fiona at arm's length. No way could he allow her to get close and pry any information out of him. With his feelings for her in turmoil, he didn't want any temptation. "Maybe I should stay at a nearby hotel. It would allow for the privacy that you want."

"No. I want you nearby, at my convenience. I feel that the situation may shift quickly. But I agree that you'll be hounded by my granddaughters. What if I moved you to the guesthouse?"

"That would be perfect." He exhaled, satisfied with his effort to keep his distance from Fiona.

"I think you're believing too quickly that you're in control of the situation between you and my granddaughter." Grace had a way of turning up the heat under Leo's collar.

"Excuse me?"

"Fiona is a stubborn and proud woman. I don't know why you broke up. Don't bother denying that you were together. Don't need to know the details. But I will say that she may not be so resolute about the separation. I sense a softening in both your attitudes. As long as my priorities don't cross with yours or hers, then I won't have to send you packing back to Grayson, Buckley and Tynesdale." From soft to hard, Grace's edict dissolved all things warm and fuzzy.

"I think that is enough of an incentive to keep my focus."

"Good. Now here is the information that I've just shared with you and additional details that should help with the search." She handed him a thin file. "And now, I'm off to go for my morning walk with Henry." With that, Grace exited the room.

Leo ignored the cold coffee close at hand and retrieved a fresh cup. He still wasn't interested in the Danish pastries. What had he stepped into with secrets, potential scandal and hopefully a happy ending for this family?

Where did that leave him when his mission had been accomplished? Would he be the hero reuniting Fiona with her brother? More important, did he want another chance to be with her? This case might push him faster than he'd ever imagined toward Fiona. On the other hand, the family's newly revealed history hadn't changed the fact that she'd dumped him.

"Fiona Reed, how am I to avoid you?" Leo gazed out the large bay window that overlooked the backyard with its garden and pool. The woman on his mind was visible outside, lounging in the shade with her e-reader. "You are bound to be my temptation."

His traitorous body flushed with desire. He was older and had better be damned wiser around her. His climb up the career ladder had been swifter than most and he liked his view. Work was even more of a priority. Anything else, Fiona included, would have to be treated like a strict diet plan. Avoid her as much as possible. If that didn't work, run as fast as he could from temptation.

Chapter 3

Fiona tried to focus on the book on her e-reader. She tried to stick with the story to figure out who'd committed the crime. But her thoughts wandered without restraint to the point that she was merely staring over the top of her e-reader. That was when she saw her grandparents walking together, completely absorbed in their animated conversation without noticing her. It took only a second to make the decision to seek out Leo. To satisfy her curiosity, nothing else.

Even if she didn't find out why he was here, she wanted to know what he'd been up to. Her conscience needled her for her desire to catch up on his life. She didn't deserve the privilege—that was more than likely what he thought. Her rationale was a bit kinder, that it could be the open door to regenerating a friendship between them.

Besides, finding out any juicy bits would shut down her cousins' silly plans to push Leo at her for debriefing. Seeing him in the flesh did bolster her openness to this second chance. The young man who had once interned at Meadows Media had morphed into a self-assured, handsome sight. His nerdy, boyish charm had evolved to well-dressed sophistication with a bit of old-Hollywood confident sex appeal.

Immediately, his intense, dark brown eyes fixed on her. She didn't look away. Couldn't. Too much to admire, from his beautiful brown skin to his clean-cut features that showed off the bold contours of his face to the tall, lean lines of his body gifted with the right muscle tone.

Stepping aside to let him focus solely on his career had been the hardest thing to do. But right before her eyes, she could see today that her decision to let him go had been for the best. Damn if it still didn't hurt like hell, though.

Seeing Leo rattled her. Although she'd anticipated his arrival, when he got out of the car, she hadn't expected the dizzying rush of emotions to race to the surface. Then seeing him in the house with only a few feet between them had had her almost hyperventilating. Outwardly, he looked unscathed by her earlier actions.

Not that she wanted to see him broken or bitter. The last image of him before they separated, as if her decision had dealt a physical blow to his gut, had become her lasting image of him.

New chapter, new beginnings—maybe that would be the theme for the reunion. Fiona stayed preoccupied, contemplating a strategy about picking up where they'd left off. Truthfully, she didn't think her attempt would be difficult, especially if he wasn't in a relationship. But after seeing him in person, the doubts weighed in her belly.

Looking into his face, those eyes staring boldly at her, she sensed the difference in him. No sign of the shy smile or tentative attitude. His cool regard of her resonated like an echo in his demeanor, expression and body language.

If it weren't for the persistent nudging from her cousins, she'd have ground out the flicker of hope and worked hard to scrub the memories of their times together once and for all.

Clicking off her e-reader, she tucked it against her chest and headed indoors. Time to get started gleaning what she could from her ex-boyfriend.

Fiona stepped inside and went on the hunt. No one was immediately in sight, although she heard activity coming from various parts of the house. As she walked down the hallway toward the staircase, she noticed luggage sitting in the middle of the entryway. Leo appeared and stopped near the parked garment bag and suitcase.

"Done with your super-secret mission? Leaving?" Fiona tried to sound nonchalant and not disappointed.

"I'm moving out to the guesthouse."

"Really? What are you up to?"

Denton entered and Fiona waited until Leo was done talking to the handyman. The guesthouse was within walking distance, but another part of the garden separated the two houses. Maybe Leo's staying off-site could be used to her advantage. He'd be out of Grace's watchful gaze. Slightly beyond her cousins' annoying interference.

"Are you going to work now? I noticed that my grandmother is off doing her own thing." Fiona motioned toward the back of the house with her chin.

"I'm going to head into town to buy a few things."

"Oh, great—I'll come with you."

"Why?"

She stuck out her hand. "Hi, I'm Fiona Reed."

He stared at her hand and then up at her face, his confusion printed in his wrinkled forehead. "Hello, Fiona." Finally he took her hand, gentle and unsure. "I'm Leo."

"Good to meet you, Leo."

"Why are we doing this?"

Fiona didn't have a clue, was just going with her gut. "That's how I greet new friends."

He slowly nodded, releasing her hand. "But we're not new friends."

"If you start from the beginning of something, it's new. Or you can fast-forward and continue with barely a ripple." She tried with every bit of effort to keep up the facade that this was a casual conversation. "Circumstances have brought us together. Figured that we can be civil, all friendly-like, as we'll be sharing the same space."

"Sounds logical." His doubt in her perspective poured out of his tone.

"I can hear the 'but' about to come. Here's the start to my peace offering. Let me drive you into town."

His eyebrows shot up.

She had to fight back a chuckle. "Hey, it's all on the up-and-up. And I know the roads around here." She crossed her heart. "I won't jump your bones." *Yet.*

Leo's smile almost emerged. "It's not that. I know

you're only interested in knowing what I'm working on."

"I won't lie that I'm not interested. Okay, very interested. However, I would like us to be on amicable terms while you're here. And if that's comfortable for you—" she paused to read him: nothing "—then we could…" Her attempts whimpered into silence.

Leo looked toward the open door. Did he want to shut this down now?

"Well, I won't push. But just wanted to toss that out to you." Fiona's pride stung around the edges.

The staircase provided her escape and she turned to leave.

"Give me an hour to get a few things settled and then we can go into the city." He stopped in the doorway.

"Hey, it's cool. Don't want to force you." Fiona wanted back on firm ground, not this squishy place of uncertainty and regret.

"You're not forcing me. Can't, really." He shrugged. "I'll take your invitation with the spirit you intended. A small step toward friendship."

"One hour, then." She watched his exit away from the tense interaction. She guessed they were in test mode. All she needed was a slight thaw in the frozen bridge between them.

Fiona headed up to her room to change her clothes. She wanted jeans and a T-shirt. Maybe dressing way down could benefit her plan to be casual and nonthreatening. As for her hair, she pulled it back into a ponytail and then put on only a light cover of makeup and an equally light sweep of lip color.

A series of short knocks on her door provided the

only heads-up that her cousins were about to barge into her room.

"Heading out?" Dana asked, unabashedly sizing up her outfit selection.

"Yeah, going out with Leo."

"That was fast. Hell, I lost the bet." Belinda pouted as she made for a chair.

Fiona rolled her eyes. "You two are of no help. I was having a hard time convincing Leo that I wanted to be friends."

"He's only playing hard to get. Why wouldn't he want to be friends?" Dana climbed onto her bed.

"The project. He thinks that I'm coming at him because I want to know what is going on," Fiona said.

"I call that being astute," Belinda remarked.

"And right," Dana interjected.

"I do want to be friends." Fiona stated her conviction for the first time to her cousins.

"For your two-week jaunt or beyond?" Dana pushed.

"You're making me sound like a calculating wench. Looks like I'll have to prove myself to Leo and to you."

"Oh, hon, no need. We're teasing." Belinda waved off her concern.

Fiona accepted the reassurance, but deep down, the teasing had a certain bite. Even Leo's cool reaction to her overture had the undercurrent of distrust. Of all the things she could be accused of, being insincere wasn't one.

Dana leaned forward from her perch on the bed. "Are you leaving soon?"

"Yeah. Why?" Fiona noticed Dana's hesitation.

"Grace wants the family together at dinner. 'It's our first night under the same roof' spiel," Dana explained.

Fiona asked, "Are my parents here?"

Belinda shook her head. "I'm guessing that they will be here by dinnertime if Grace is requesting that we all be there."

Fiona wasn't confident on that front. A glance at the clock on the mantelpiece over the fireplace let her know that it was time to meet Leo. After checking her face in the mirror and feeling satisfied with her reflection, she breezed past her cousins and headed out of the room.

"Don't do anything I'd do." Dana laughed over her witty remark.

"I'm going on instinct. No promises."

"I feel sorry for that guy." Belinda shook her head again, her mouth curved in a grin.

Fiona ran down the stairs and hit the outdoors. At that moment, Leo pulled up in his car and waited for her. Taking a deep breath and exhaling some of her nervousness, she pasted on a bright smile.

Leo beckoned to her.

She slipped on her sunglasses and headed toward the car.

Leo opened the door and she slid in. "I was going to drive." She looked up at him as she pulled the seat belt over her body.

"That's because you thought you were going to take charge of the situation." He winked before he closed the door.

She bit her cheek to stop from grinning.

Leo had changed. He was in the driver's seat, ready to take charge. She settled back in her seat to enjoy the ride.

After a lengthy silence during the drive, he asked, "What should we talk about? Where should we start?"

Fiona appreciated his effort to make the first move or set the marker for where they should begin the new stage. "Work, maybe? You're an associate lawyer now. Congratulations on the achievement. I knew you would do it."

"It was one of my dreams."

"Still is, I hope. You're good at it."

He glanced at her. "Not that I don't appreciate the confidence, but how would you know?"

"You work for my grandmother. She doesn't settle for second-best. That's how I know."

"She does know what she wants." His voice trailed and his attention was no longer on Fiona.

"But sometimes what she wants might not be wanted by others." Fiona turned her gaze to the scenery outside the window.

Fiona considered her childhood stable and consistent. Strains and tensions had occasionally filtered into her family life, but she viewed all interactions and relationships as normal. Even her cousins had their fair share of family challenges.

Lately, however, those pesky vibes appeared to be on the rise. Or more troubling was that for the first time she saw her grandmother worry and hearing that Grandpa Henry seemed to be at odds with his wife. Not that his opinion had never strayed from Grace's, but he'd always put on a brave face and supported her 100 percent.

"I can't tell you," he said without looking at her.

Fiona didn't respond. Without knowing the subject matter, she had no idea what direction to aim her questions. For now, she'd relax into the seat and enjoy the afternoon.

"What about your job? Still a kick-ass detective?"

"Yep. It keeps me going." She would have gushed that her job was like the oxygen she needed to function if she wouldn't have come across as too intense.

"I bet you still work those long hours."

"Like you. Remember how we'd end up having to call for Chinese-food delivery?" Fiona hoped that the happier times mattered to him, too.

"I did cook a meal or two sometimes." Leo's smile was pure heaven. "Had you asking for seconds."

Not the only thing that she'd asked for seconds of.

She shot a glance his way to admire his strong profile. Her thumb used to press against those full lips that, when curled into a smile, created a dimple on the right side, close to the bottom corner of his lip. She'd kiss that spot until he gave in to her demands. The flashback fueled a hot flush in her belly. Her hands ran the length of her thighs as she focused on Leo.

"What about you? Are you still grabbing food on the run?" he asked.

"Yeah, I guess." She smoothed any loose hair into place and rested her head against her propped hand. "Sometimes the work has a way of taking over your life."

"You always gave it your all. All in or all out."

She sensed that the judgment didn't pertain to work. "Finding missing loved ones or even people ignored or discarded by society is important to me. Maybe it didn't start out that way, like a calling that comes from the heart." She broke off with an embarrassed laugh. "Sorry. Again, my intensity is my downfall."

He laid a gentle hand over hers on her lap. "Your intensity…is attractive."

Boom. The nerves in her body sparked to life like the flickering hum of fluorescent bulbs turning on.

She slid her hand from under his. That wasn't any better, with his hand now resting on her lap. But thankfully, he returned it to the steering wheel. Her lap would have been lit up with a fiery glow under an infrared light.

She took a deep breath and attempted a better explanation. "I transferred over to the Missing Persons Unit because it was less maneuvering and clawing up the career ladder. It had the reputation for being the place where the close-to-retirement and those who had screwed up went to finish their years with the department. Plus, it's a small staff, working on a tight budget." Her anger was still fresh over the latest reduction in funds and freezing of pay raises. "Anyway, I get my stack of cases and I go to work."

"Are there a lot of happy endings?"

"Only in the movies. How soon the person is reported missing and how fast we can coordinate with the various local entities determine the success rates. But I do get a lot of cases where we know who has the child. Those would be the custody battles. Or the grandparent who is looking out for the best interest of the child. However, they don't have official guardianship. Starts as a missing persons case and evolves into other major crimes as more information is revealed."

"The grind of the job has got to be a bummer, though. You don't eat. You don't take vacation. Actually, I'm surprised to see you without a gun at your side. You're the role of the avenging angel."

"I do eat," she protested.

"Okay. Last Monday… Can you remember that long ago?" he teased, the tiny dimple appearing.

"Last Monday…" she repeated, waiting for an indication of where this conversation was heading.

"What did you have for breakfast? No dressing up the truth, either."

She didn't have to think about it. Her breakfast was always the same. And it would sound inadequate.

"I'm waiting."

"Hot water with lemon. But it helps to start the day and energize the body."

"I think that's for the meal that is supposed to follow. So go ahead—you have your zero-calorie water and go to work. Then what?"

"I have a coffee. Two donuts."

"What's in the desk drawer?" His questions shot out at her.

"Twizzlers."

"And lunch?"

"I usually eat…"

"We're talking about Monday."

Fiona huffed. "I skipped lunch, but only because I had a lead on a case involving twins. I had to check it out. You can't expect that I would sit down for a meal when two young girls were in danger of being part of a sex trafficking ring."

"And after you checked out the lead?"

"It was late afternoon. I had paperwork to finish on some other cases. Another department was waiting on my report. I couldn't just stop to eat."

"And how many Twizzler bags did you go through?"

"Pleading the Fifth." She bit her lip to keep from laughing.

"And when you're home. Late. Hungry. Tired. Is someone there to make you dinner?"

She chuckled. "Um…are you asking me if I have a special someone in my life who cooks me wonderful meals that make me ask for seconds?"

"Certainly not." He turned his head, but not before she saw the tug of a smile.

"Well, for dinner I called for a pizza. By the time it was delivered, I'd fallen asleep on the couch. I took the pizza, dropped it on the table and went to sleep on the couch until Tuesday morning to start the day again. But that morning I did grab a slice of the pizza on my way out the door. A solid breakfast, if you ask me."

"If you keep eating like that, you will get sick or flat-out faint on the job. You won't be good to anyone."

"Aren't you the concerned one?" She looked over at him to see if there were any signs that he was truly worried. His expression didn't reveal such clues.

"You can still do what you need to do and be kind to yourself."

"If you read those missing-persons files, saw pictures of the ones that aren't found in the best of shapes, you might understand."

He parked the car, turned off the engine and hovered, as if something weighed on him.

But the silence loaded with emotion and expectation unnerved her. She unsnapped her seat belt, opened the door and practically fell out to get into the open air, the wider space. Sitting next to him, his shoulder within reach of her head to rest on and his cologne to play with her memory of his signature scent, stirred her regret. There was no room for remorse when she'd made the decision to cut ties with Leo.

She had been twenty-nine; he had been twenty-five, fresh out of law school with the world in front of him to claim. Their attraction had been so intense, heady and all-consuming that it had taken every bit of resolve for her to step away from their relationship. How could she be the one to block him from experiencing life? He hadn't lived yet. Hadn't started his legal career. Hadn't even taken the bar exam.

Maybe because of opportunity and her family, she'd lived a life of privilege that was beyond her years. She'd jumped into experiences. Some didn't need to be repeated or remembered, but she went off with no concerns and no one to feel obligated to.

So despite how much she had fallen for this younger man, and how much she'd wanted a life with him, and how much he'd gotten past her defenses and into her heart, she'd made the tough choice. To this day, she debated that she'd done the right thing, even if it ached like a physical wound.

"Would you tell me about the last case…the twins?" He rounded the car and waited for her to join him on the sidewalk.

She walked beside him. They headed toward Main Street, where the small boutique shops were now opening. The streets were still fairly empty as the town slowly got active on the Sunday afternoon.

"The twins were a special case. I try not to think about the cases after I'm done working on them. I even have a ritual after I'm done with the file. It helps me to move on."

He didn't say anything, but she knew he was paying close attention. She'd always liked the way he actively listened to her. When she had her rants, when she got excited, when she wanted to talk about the world's problems, no matter what, he'd quietly listen.

"My ritual is a bit silly. No matter the outcome, when I find my missing person, and after I finish the paperwork, I send them off with a prayer. I want them to be at peace. I want them to be protected. I pray that they know love and acceptance after such a terrible ordeal."

"I think that's something very special, kind and necessary."

"And for the ones that I don't find, I commit their names to my heart. And I don't ever stop following tips and leads. Sometimes they come to me in my dreams." She'd slowed, coming to a stop. Emotions welled. "The twins...that was rough." She blinked away the tears, pushing back the nightmares that haunted her. "I can't talk about them yet."

No sound between them. Only the rustle of the breeze blowing debris, the tires of a bicycle on the cobbled street, the tinkle of a bell as a shop door opened and closed filled the space around them. Her hair that escaped from the ponytail blew into her face, partially shielding her view of Leo's reaction. She didn't know why what he thought was something that she wanted to know. But it was.

She'd missed when he stepped closer. But he was there in front of her. His hand gently harnessed the wayward hair and guided it behind her ear. The softness of his palm rested against her cheek. Her breath quickened. Just a slight turn, and she could press her lips into his hand. She closed her eyes to regain her sanity.

"I'm here whenever you want to talk." His voice had

always had a rich huskiness with his Brazilian accent. His caring words bathed her in a warm glow.

"How about we get some ice cream?" Fiona took two determined steps back, away from the invitation of his body and out of reach of his hand.

"Ice cream it is." He opened the door of a tiny store and waved her in. "I hope that your appetite won't get screwed up for Grace's dinner tonight. I'm not taking responsibility."

"I promise to eat everything on my plate." She held up her hand in a mock pledge.

The ice-cream shop was the perfect diversion from the heavy, maudlin thoughts that she didn't want to air to anyone. The impulsive act of joining Leo wasn't supposed to be a therapy session for her. She had handled her demons on her own and didn't need anyone rattling around in her fears to make things worse.

"I am officially extending an open dinner invitation to you. Whenever you'd like, I will cook a fantastic meal." Leo surprised her with his offer as they left the shop.

"Hmm."

"You have to think about it?"

"Just wondering if you invite a lot of women to your home with a tasty meal as the lure." She had to say what was on her mind, what she needed to know.

"I'm pretty much a private soul. These days, I only want to spend my free time with friends."

"Ah...I'm back in the friend slot."

He chuckled.

Fiona would take another small step into the thaw. Hopefully, the ground would stay firm as she tentatively tested her way back into Leo's life.

Their pace picked up and now they entered an open-air market. This was the main attraction point, with people pouring into the area to drift off to the various booths. He seemed to know what he wanted to buy as he led the way to several stalls and chatted with the owners. His scrutiny landed on the best fruits and vegetables. Before long they had several bags between them. Yet he refused to say what this grand meal would be.

"It felt good to get away," she said on their way back to the car.

"You just got here."

"Yeah, but I'm sort of a solitary soul. It takes a bit of getting used to having everyone around you every day," she confessed.

"When I was younger, I wanted to be part of a large family."

"I'm an only child. We're similar in that way."

Leo didn't say anything. But she saw the shadow that descended over him. They reached the car and still he hadn't said anything further. They pulled off and headed out of the downtown to return to the estate.

Fiona didn't want this friendly exchange to end or get stymied upon their return. She pushed softly, "You've met most of my family. I've never met yours." Fiona checked the solemn profile to see his reaction. "I know you're from Brazil. I know you lived in Massachusetts. And now you're in New York."

"My journey to this point is…" His hands gripped the steering wheel. His jaw worked. "It was hard. My mother died. My father came to Brazil, married, and abandoned the family before I was born." He shrugged off a burden that she was sure never lifted.

"I'm sorry."

"My entire family was swept away in a massive flood. The rerouting of a dam left the village at risk. It was a flash flood that plowed through the land, ripping up everything in its path. We were asleep. There was no warning. In the dark, I tried to find my four older brothers and little sister."

"Oh no…" Fiona couldn't imagine that level of devastation.

"It wasn't just my family. But over three-quarters of the village population, mainly children, died. People mourned. The government made a mediocre apology with some funding. But life was never the same. And religious ministries and charities took on the heavy lifting to give the orphans some type of stability, even if it meant relocating them. A family adopted me when I was twelve years old."

"What about your father?"

"He was never on my birth certificate. He'd never been in my mother's life long enough to know of me. My Brazilian family name is Ribeiro."

"And Leo…was that your name?"

"Leonardo. But Leo was what my mother called me."

"Have you ever gone back to Brazil?"

He shook his head. "No, this is home now. It's where you put down your feet and live. Brazil is in my blood. That's enough for me."

"I hope that one day you do reconnect with someone from your family." She sincerely hoped he did get rediscover his roots.

"I love the Starks family in Massachusetts who adopted me. I'm content."

"Oh, I didn't mean that you should turn your back on them. But there might be an aunt or uncle out there. Hoping for the best." She didn't want to sound like an insensitive boob.

"Hope is an expensive hanger-on." He spoke with a startling flatness.

"You used to have a lot of hope." Fiona realized that she hadn't been wrong when she'd sensed his frosty emotional condition. It didn't appear to be deeply buried. Or she brought out this side of him. A sobering thought.

"And look where that got me." He pulled up in front of the house with a sharp pump on the brake that had them both lurching forward and falling back into their seats.

"Hope shouldn't ever be discarded." She didn't know how to ease his bitterness.

"Blind faith is for the young."

"Now you're trying to convince me that your twenty-eight years have moved you into Confucius status? What does that make me at thirty-two? And watch what you say, or I'm not coming to your dinner party."

That seemed to tone down the heated exchange.

He stared straight ahead. His jaw working over whatever thoughts wrestled behind his mental curtain. Then he turned to her with a half smile and replied, "I wouldn't want to do that. Wouldn't want you not to feel welcome."

Fiona watched his smile unfold into something warm and achingly familiar. Right now, if he leaned over to initiate the hint of a kiss, she would fall under his spell. Her plan was to navigate the bumpy road between them, staying away from the ragged potholes that could cause a snag in their momentum toward a fragile truce. What her plan didn't take into account was how strong her desire for Leo was.

She could keep the peace with a neutral, friendly approach. Or she could surrender to her powerful yearning and blast the landscape to smithereens.

As she looked up into his eyes, his unreadable reaction made her hesitate over what to do. But since when had she become so cautious?

Fiona took a deep breath and mentally jumped off the cliff. Just like that, she decided to free-fall and go with the unpredictable, risky scenario. Perform a sneak attack and go after, for the second time, the only man she ever loved.

Chapter 4

The call to dinner had the power to tie Leo's stomach into nervous knots. Time to meet the rest of the family. Normally, vacation settings called for a casual get-together for the average family coming to eat at the dinner table. But this event didn't feel casual at all. Plus, this wasn't the average family. As the outsider, he hoped to stay quietly on the periphery without affecting the family dynamic. There was enough gossip about rivalries and strained relationships between Grace and her children that he didn't want to witness any drama during his stay. His goal was to attend to Grace's business needs and smoothly navigate through any awkward dilemmas. And he felt sure there would be more than a few, especially with Fiona's ability to twist his common sense into a chaotic mess, along with being a conspirator in keeping a huge family secret.

His rising guilt rustled like a persistent, soft breeze over dry, brittle land, stirring up the top layer of dirt. With an effort, he relied on cold, plain logic to tamp down the pangs.

"Ah, good to see that you're quite prompt, Leo." Grace was already seated in the dining room at the head of the table. Her head bobbed in a regal nod.

She introduced him to Felicity and Wade, Belinda's parents. Then he met Cassie—Grace's sister—and Elaine, who was Dana's mother. Familiarizing himself with the family tree was an important survival step. Grace's husband, Henry, waved from the opposite head seat at the table. Leo settled for the chair diagonally opposite Fiona's to avoid being obvious when he stole glances at her.

An invisible dividing line through the middle of the table separated the past and the present generations. Grace's daughters and their spouses sat facing each other, closer to her side. At the other end, the grand-daughters and Jesse clustered together with Henry. Leo figured his seat close to the middle line was Switzerland and he'd do his best to stay in neutral territory. A quick look at Fiona, who caught his peek, and his body reacted as if hit with static electricity, a reminder that he was anything but neutral.

The generational division was also on display in their outward appearances. Parents showed up to dinner suited up and dressed in their Sunday best. The granddaughters, except for Dana, who was missing, wore casual to, well, dressy casual. He couldn't tell if the younger generation aimed to be deliberately rebellious. But he suspected that they knew their strength was in their unity.

Leo relied on simple logic for interacting with the Meadowses on their turf. Since he was the guest, and not really on vacation, he chose to observe, play by the rules and fight to come out on the winning side of any game. While his white shirt, minus a tie, and black pants couldn't be mistaken as formal wear or designer casual, he did earn Grace's nod of approval.

As the family's cornerstone, Grace was the long-serving reigning queen. Even the afternoon sun seemed to collaborate with her to accentuate her power. The slanted beam of sunlight shone through the large windows and over Grace's chair. Bathed in its glow, she looked the part of the matriarch in a simple but classic soft white dress. She looked down the length of the table with a gracious smile.

"Hey, Grandma, Grandpa, everyone else. Can't wait to dig in." Dana sailed through the door in capri pants and a T-shirt. She didn't look anything like the CEO of a media company.

"Why must you be so loud?" Grace openly regarded her choice of clothing, which Dana ignored as she weighed her options for an open seat.

Her gaze settled on the seat next to Leo. The wide grin directed at him made him feel like a trap had been set. "Hi, Leo, how was your date with Fiona? Oops, did I say *date*? I mean *day*."

Leo cringed, refusing to look at the head of the table. Could her voice be any louder?

Dana leaned in toward him. "Well…?"

"It wasn't a date. We drove into town for a few things." He kept his voice low, but the sudden quietness around the table easily lifted his words to ensure that everyone heard his abrupt denial.

"Either way, I'd say that you have a girlfriend." Dana didn't let up. She rubbed his nerves like an annoying a younger sibling—or like he imagined an annoying younger sibling would.

"Dana, stop with your foolishness. Say the prayer," Grace ordered.

"Maybe that'll shut her up," Fiona said, with an accompanying death stare at her cousin.

The prayer before meals was offered and was followed by two servants entering with the first course, French-onion soup. Leo didn't eat like this, where his meals came in seemingly nonstop waves. He hoped that it wouldn't be bad manners not to finish everything on his plate. This wasn't the place to gorge and sit back afterward, patting his full belly.

As he left his soup bowl with half its contents, he heard Fiona's slight clearing of her throat. He looked up to see her exaggeratedly scooping the last bit of her soup from the bowl and into her mouth. She offered a slight nod. Shifting his gaze back to his bowl, he conceded that she was eating a full meal. Without making eye contact, he lifted the corner of his mouth as acknowledgment of her effort.

The second round of food smelled mouthwateringly good. The covered dish was placed in front of him. Steam jutted from the hole in the center of the dome. He wanted to rub his hands and bounce in his chair like a kid waiting to open presents. His stomach rumbled loud enough for Dana to giggle. The server pulled off the cover.

Leo inhaled the rich savory smell of filet mignon, roasted red potatoes and steamed artichoke tips. He had no doubt that a master chef worked in the kitchen. The presentation was perfection. His mouth was already anticipating the first bite. Good grief, he didn't want to be the first to attack the plate, but his restraint was on the verge of collapse. He couldn't wait to dive in.

Raised voices and a hurried clatter of footsteps approaching the dining room interrupted his plan to cut into the tender meat. His first glance was at Grace, who visibly bristled, her attention glued to the doorway. For some clue as to what was happening, he ignored Dana and looked over to Fiona for enlightenment. She was half-turned in the seat with her gaze also on the doorway. Although he couldn't see her expression, her body language offered enough clues that the arriving guests caused the rigid set of her shoulders and the tension in her face. A harried man appeared in the room before a woman, whose visage and attitude had an ice-queen edge, stepped into view alongside him.

Dana leaned in toward him. "It's Fiona's mother, Verona, and her father, Jasper. They've come fashionably late. Not their style, but I guess something more important must have held them up. Uncle Jasper looks like he's going to have a stroke. He's all about punctuality. Aunt Verona, not so much."

Leo appreciated the intel. He didn't want to sit in the chair of judgment on this woman who had a secret that was soon to be no longer hers. But he couldn't stop his mind from wondering about her as she moved with fluid grace farther into the room. This woman who oozed confidence and haughty disdain didn't mesh with the story of a young mother in college who'd successfully hidden her pregnancy.

"Mother, sorry we are late. Jasper had work to complete at the office before we could leave to get here."

She brushed her cheek against her mother's and then headed down to the other side of the table to kiss her father's cheek. "Fiona, good to see you." She touched her daughter's shoulder but pulled back as soon as her hand landed, as if she'd suddenly realized what she'd done.

Verona raised her eyes, locking on to him with glacial precision.

He had to display grit, even if he had to fake the steely resolve. It shouldn't be a shock that he wouldn't be showered with warm smiles and consideration. The details of his assignment dictated the landscape be unfriendly and frosty.

Fiona's noticeable hurt at Verona's stiff greeting did throw him off. The obvious emotional turmoil between mother and daughter was unexpected. But Fiona had never shared much about her parents. And as he recalled, she'd never introduced him to them. While Verona did a good impression of an ice princess, Jasper murmured his hellos to everyone, nodding to him but staying put in his seat. Overall, he looked exhausted.

"Verona, would you take your seat so we can continue with our meal?" Grace's irritation pinged off each word.

Finally, Leo dived into his food. Maybe the steak wasn't piping hot, but it was still deliciously edible. Eating was a lot easier on the digestion than watching this display.

"You were saying, Leo, that you went to the market with Fiona." Dana pressed on and he dearly wanted to stab her hand with the fork. Any points she'd earned for the intel had been subtracted for the relentless teasing. Couldn't she read the massive spike of tension in the room?

"Oh, leave it alone." Fiona burst into the discussion. "Stop making something out of nothing."

Silence dropped for few seconds before forks sharply hit a plate or two. Leo kept his head down and admired the perfectly cut stems of the artichoke.

"Jesse, how are the renovations with the stable going? More expansion, right?" Henry took the baton and Leo wanted to offer a hearty handshake to the older man.

"Yes, sir. The clients have doubled after the opening ceremony." Thanks to Jesse's prompt response, silence didn't hang over the group. Various conversations continued.

Henry said, "Good. I think children should have a place to come and have fun. Life is too serious."

"It's not really a playground, Grandpa. It's so that children with disabilities and challenges, physical or otherwise, can receive another form of therapy. Using horses isn't a new method to treat people. My goal is to make it more accessible." Belinda's passion poured out in a way that caught Leo's interest in her endeavor.

"I didn't mean to offend you, dear."

"I know. And I didn't mean to sound like a walking billboard."

They continued talking about the center, with more family members now contributing to the discussion. As they shared their insights, Leo realized how unique they were and the common base was their innovative mind-set. He wasn't familiar with Grace's daughters, but they had to have learned something from their mother to have raised their own daughters to make their marks in their respective careers. That generational legacy was an aching void in his life.

"Grace, you really haven't introduced your guest." An unfamiliar female voice shifted the conversation to his presence.

Leo looked up from his almost-empty plate and toward the voice to see who had turned on the spotlight and pointed it on him. Every face looked back at him.

"Sorry, I thought everyone knew Leo. Cassie, he is working on some legal matters that couldn't wait until after our vacation. He's staying in the guesthouse, but you will see him in my office. Please make him feel welcomed, everyone."

Grace's sister regarded him without hostility but with such open curiosity that he wanted to ask her if something was wrong. He doubted that Cassie was satisfied by Grace's explanation.

"I'm sure Fiona will be happy to make him feel comfortable," Dana mumbled for only his ears.

"And that would make her kind." Leo didn't mumble or mutter. After dispatching his message, he fed himself the last piece of steak.

Grace cleared her throat, a signal for their collective attention. "It is my hope that before we go back to our daily lives after our family vacation, I'll have good news to share with you."

Verona's cutlery clattered against the china. "Excuse me, everyone—it's been a long day. I'll head up to the room now." She didn't wait for Grace's acknowledgment but, clearly upset, hurried from the room, trailed by her husband.

Leo turned toward Fiona, whose gaze tracked her mother's abrupt departure from the dining room. He expected her to follow. She didn't. Instead Fiona directed her confusion at her grandmother. But Grace either ignored Fiona or didn't focus on her as she silently communicated with her husband across the table.

Meanwhile, none of them knew that Leo was the key to unlocking this mystery. His role would open a door for the family that could never be closed again. The depth of his responsibility filled him with unease that Grace was stirring up something that would rock the foundation of her own inner sanctum.

Yet he wouldn't be immune from the fallout. His role as the igniter of the explosion likely would do irrevocable damage between Fiona and him. Never in his life had he felt such a burden to do his job.

No doubt they'd label him an agitator. All he could hope was that Fiona would appreciate what her grandmother was trying to do and understand what her mother had done.

As for himself, he didn't hold out much hope. Leo sucked in a deep breath and exhaled. He had to keep his mind on the job and keep the door locked on his feelings that could compromise his duties.

"Grandma, can you give us a hint?" Belinda chose to be the one to push the matter.

"No. And stop nagging me or your grandfather." Despite the scolding, Grace's tone was surprisingly gentle.

Henry raised his hand in surrender. "My lips are on lockdown."

Dana poked Leo's thigh. "What about you? Do you have your lips on lockdown?"

Leo didn't know if telling the CEO of Meadows Media to be quiet would have soaring repercussions, but he was willing to risk it.

He leaned over to her, looking straight into her eyes. "Please let me know where you'll be sitting for the next meal. I want you to enjoy your food in a way that I wasn't able to do."

"Don't worry—I'll let dear sweet Fiona have my seat. And I'll take hers. But warning—I do know how to read lips."

"When is Kent coming to the estate? Obviously you need another distraction." Fiona glared at her younger cousin. "That would be the reason for you to be so annoyingly bratty at dinner to our guest."

"Well, I…I was just teasing and trying to see what Leo was made of. No need to get all hot and bothered, both of you." She did look sheepish. "Sorry."

Leo nodded but knew better than to think Dana had turned a corner with her behavior toward him. Before his time was over here, he wanted to get to know her, as difficult as it would be. Being on the right side of the cousins had to count in his favor if he entertained the slimmest possibility of a reconciliation with Fiona.

When the servers appeared in the room to remove dishes, Grace instructed, "You may serve the dessert before these *children* lose any more self-control."

The servers promptly returned with a platter of tiny desserts that they set along the middle of the table. Sugar and spices filled his nostrils with their enticing scents. Mini pies, slices of cakes and small tarts taunted his willpower. The colorful array of treats brought a stop to the bickering. The mood lightened considerably as everyone consumed the desserts and now chatted about the trending news of the day.

By the time Leo was done, he couldn't have taken on another meal if one came on a chariot for him. He complimented Grace and the serving staff profusely. Still he didn't know how he'd suffer under the caloric intake if he stayed here too long. Jogging might have to become part of his daily routine.

"See you bright and early in the morning, Leo. We'll get started right away." Grace turned her attention to Henry. In other words, Leo was dismissed.

He had to admit that he was glad to escape to the guesthouse. A good meal—yes. His nerves—no. Hanging around the cousins with a possible resumption of Dana's constant digs wasn't how he wanted to spend the remainder of the night. And he didn't know Jesse well enough to suggest another option, like a drink and a game of cards. His best bet was a speedy retreat.

Before he'd entered this house, his nerves were on edge. Now sitting in the midst of the Meadows family dynamics in full play, he needed some time to himself. Every time he looked up, he couldn't help but check out Fiona. Sometimes, he wanted her reaction. Sometimes, he simply wanted to look at her. The warm flush over his body wasn't the appropriate response for watching her eat, admiring her throat as she drank from her glass, or being ready to squirm in his seat as she occasionally dabbed at the corners of her mouth. Maintaining an image of calm took so much effort on his part.

"Want to go for a walk?" Fiona had quietly approached to stand by his side.

"In the dark?" Leo waved the surrender flag to his manufactured neutrality. Beyond the immediate perimeter of the house, the property blended into the darkness. Privacy felt more like isolation after sundown.

Being alone with Fiona…he remembered those times with vivid recollection. His heart pounded a tad harder, a tad faster.

"There's a small garden that leads to a glass gazebo.

It's nice to sit in there and watch the fireflies." She coaxed him with a tender smile. "I used to do that as a kid. Sit in there when I was supposed to be sleeping. I guess that sounds a bit childish." Her head bowed, the embarrassed smile swaying his decision.

"No, not childish at all. I'd like that. Great way to wind down after dinner." The time he'd spent with Fiona today had set them on a good path. And he wanted that to continue after the tension-laden dinner.

They headed out one of the back doors that led right to the patio. Their feet crunched along the tiny stones that paved the path around the sculpted gardens. Microlights that lit the footpath turned on upon their approach. The suffused lights gave an ethereal glow to the surrounding plants and blossoming flowers.

"Sorry about Dana. She's not usually like that and I'm not usually yelling at her. I felt like we were back to being teenagers again. Everyone is acting wonky, if you ask me."

He shrugged. "I think we came to an understanding."

"I don't know what you said, but she did seem to correct her attitude." Fiona playfully jabbed him with her elbow. "Call it a vibe, but we know that whatever it is doesn't sit well between my grandparents. Feels like a heavy cloud holding steady over our heads ready to burst at any moment. That feeling is rare. And if it's business-related about Meadows, then Grace is meddling and has shut out Dana. All of this secrecy is not good, because it's causing friction."

Leo listened to her concerns with complete understanding. If she only knew that it wasn't about the work, except that someone would be added to the will.

Despite all the rumors about Grace's tight hold on the reins of the family, there had never been any talk about financial issues. No bad apples who spent money outrageously or needed to be bailed out for acts of stupidity. However, the big reveal of an additional grandchild was one thing. Sharing the family wealth with this person might be another.

All the potential drama didn't matter, because he couldn't offer any clues. "Have you ever been able to make your grandmother do something that she didn't want to do?"

"Are you kidding? No way."

"Then maybe everyone needs to relax and give her some space." Leo wanted to change the subject.

"Aren't you the advocate?" she ribbed. "Grace would be proud."

"Don't make me have to say it—can't we all get along?"

She lightheartedly bumped his shoulder. "No matter how much we bicker, I do love my family. Every quirky character belongs."

Her touch on his skin zapped him like an unexpected buzz of static shock. After going out of his way to avoid teasing his senses with her closeness, his efforts had been for nothing. The playful contact only had him yearning for more.

"I know you do." He raised his hand to place it around her shoulders but restrained himself and dropped his hand to his side. "I wished that I'd been able to meet them...back in the day."

She looked down and he couldn't read her. A soft sigh escaped. "I wasn't ready."

The simple confession tapped at the wall he'd put

up and tried to defend against her invasion. He didn't mind easing into a friendship, but he was determined to keep the wall intact. Guarding his heart mattered. Maintaining the emotional distance would help him and her, for when the truth was revealed about his assignment.

He hoped that she remembered how much she loved her family.

He hoped that she'd believe in him and trust his judgement.

"We're here." Fiona pulled open the door of the gazebo.

Just like the footpath lights that lit up when motion was detected, the ones in the gazebo turned on. The door closed, shutting out the sounds of nature. Lights in the glass house weren't bright but instead produced a soft, muted ambiance that lent the notion of a romantic mood. A suite of chairs and a center table furnished the space. The rest of the walls of the gazebo had a bench lining the semicircle shape of the building.

Fiona walked around the circular structure. "I can see your place from here."

He stood next to her. Regardless of whether they were in the bright light of the day, like earlier, or in the subdued light of this building now, his close presence always had her taking deep breaths to regulate the jumpy spikes to her pulse. Hot coals would have to be placed in the inner linings of her clothes to match the intensity of her feelings and sweet craving for him. She wanted to take a small side step and allow her arm to lightly press against his.

"It's a really neat and small house for visiting guests."

"When I was younger, I thought that I'd live there."

"Why would you want to when you've got all of this?" He pointed toward the main house.

"It's huge. I like my privacy."

"It's beautiful." His compliment felt personal.

"It's big," she countered.

"It has class and elegance."

"It's a statement," Fiona volleyed back.

"It's a legacy."

Fiona had no comeback. Since her birth, the Meadows name and legacy had been the magical password for her life and privilege. Striking out on her own to be independent wasn't a total disengagement when she spent vacations in the Hamptons. The two sides to her life battled with her conscience, as if she had something to apologize for while also being thankful for what her grandmother had accomplished.

When she'd met Leo, she'd done her best to push all the trappings out of the picture. She knew he was a hungry lawyer and she didn't want her family connections to be the attraction instead of her. But Leo had never been that sort. Now she recognized that. Back then, she hadn't necessarily given him the benefit of the doubt.

She turned to study his profile. Bold and contoured, his razor-sharp jawline defined the shape of his face. She remembered those intimate moments, after rousing sex, when she'd trace the lines and angles of his face with her eyes closed. Her fingers moved as if she played a piano at her side. She sucked in her bottom lip.

Brown skin against winter-white sheets.

His chest was wide and chiseled. The perfect pillow for her to lay her head on.

Her nipples tightened. They were usually pressed against his side as she cuddled in bed under his arm draped down her body. Somehow his hand always rested on the curve of her behind. She was his. He was hers.

"What I prefer is over there." She gestured toward the guesthouse, when she'd rather have pointed her finger at him.

"That simple house?" He looked in its direction.

"Simple is sexy."

"That's the first that I've heard a house called sexy."

"Maybe I'm not talking about the house." Fiona inhaled the waft of his cologne. She closed her eyes to intensify the sensation. The way he said *sexy*—that was sexy.

"Are you flirting with me?" His eyes were hooded. His voice dropped deep into his chest.

"See, I've always liked that you're so smart. I find that…refreshing."

"Flirting won't get me to tell you anything."

Fiona shook her head. "Two separate issues. One's business. The other's pleasure."

"Not sure I can keep each one in its own box." His head turned away, leaving her with only his profile.

"Shouldn't be difficult. You're not the enemy for either cause."

Leo didn't answer.

"Am I stepping into someone else's territory?"

He shook his head.

"Then let's go with the flow."

"That's how we got started. Going with your flow."

His accusation attached itself squarely on Fiona's shoulders.

"Then let's go with your flow, your pace, your parameters," she responded with quiet determination.

That drew his attention, more like a flat stare that almost had her squirmy under his scrutiny.

He said, "You so easily trust me? What about my revenge? What if I took your heart and shredded it without losing sleep?"

"That's not who you are." Fiona knew she'd hurt him. But she'd convinced herself that he wanted his career more than her. "You didn't live in the Meadows family unit. So you haven't witnessed the critical moment when we must decide if it will be Meadows Media or our personal career aspirations. From my cousins' and my experience, I get how tough it can be to be sidelined from what you want to do. Guilt and a feeling of obligation can wreck the desire to stay the course. Even the idea of being true to your heart and remaining somewhat independent can cause some restless nights. And I didn't want that for you."

"You decided for me," Leo accused with soft resignation.

Fiona rushed with her explanation. "I learned early in my career how to spot potential liabilities and make the hard decisions."

"When you could have just taken the effort to really get to know me."

"Then give me a chance." She tucked in the ragged edges of her pride and shame. "Please give me a second chance."

"One day at a time."

"Can't ask for anything more," Fiona said, knowing that her heart wanted more.

He offered his hand. "Friends."

"To lovers." She shook his hand, afraid that he would withdraw and tuck it behind his back.

"You're quite persuasive."

"We don't have too many days here. Figured that if you wouldn't persuade me, then it's up to me."

"Yeah? Go ahead. Persuade."

Fiona didn't waste another second. She slipped her hands around Leo's neck and stood on tiptoe to reach his mouth.

One kiss. One mouth pressed against the other. That was all it was.

Except, when she kissed Leo, she wanted more. She desired him.

Breathe.

Once more she reacquainted her lips with his beautiful wide mouth, tracing its bold curves. Celebrating its masculine lines.

As if touched by magic, time stood still. Meanwhile, every nerve in her body sparked to life, their vibrations humming in tune with his powerful sexual vibes.

His arms encircled her waist, pulling her against his hardness. She gasped and sucked in air through her clenched teeth. His hands rested on the top of her behind, keeping his hips pressed against hers.

No doubt he was aroused—thick and rigid.

No doubt she was wet.

Their breathing intermingled. Their bodies were clasped in each other's arms. Fiona went with the urge. "I want you." She shook her head. "I want you so bad that I can't think."

He closed his eyes. His chest rose and fell as if he'd run up the staircase at full speed. "Now? Or somewhere more private?"

Fiona didn't want him to toy with her. "Both." This wasn't the time for his neutrality.

He kissed her hard. Waves of lust slammed her. Her knees trembled with her surrender. Moving her hands from around his body, he pinned them behind her back with one hand. Her breath hitched and grew erratic as his other hand traced the fullness of her breasts. His mouth didn't let up. After a bruising kiss to her chin, it followed its scorched path down through the valley of her breasts.

She arched up, moaning her submission. Having his hands all over her body was definitely in the forecast. Her clothes were a hindrance. Under the night sky, she'd gladly rip off everything. Or she'd have him take his time undressing her. Either way was a win.

An outside light near the door of the house turned on, breaking the moment. They didn't dare move in case the lights in the gazebo turned back on.

Instead Fiona gently raised her head, lifting him away from her breasts. "Were we saved by an interrupter?" She laughed, but it came out as a rueful whimper. "You offered friendship and I took it and ran to the finish line. Maybe I should head back inside." She hated to be reasonable, but couldn't help the automatic pump on the brakes. A cautious approach was an ingrained habit.

"You didn't do anything that I didn't want to happen."

"Still, we should head to our respective corners. Tomorrow is another day."

"Sounds like a plan." He was breathing hard.

"I don't want Grace to know what may be going on." Well, actually, she didn't want anyone to know. If there would be a second chance, she didn't want the scrutiny if anything went wrong.

"She already does."

"What?" Fiona groaned at what this would mean for Leo.

"She put it out there that she suspected we had something going on."

Fiona dropped her head in her hands. With the shift away from the dangerously sexy mood, she didn't mind triggering the automatic lights. "And what did you say?"

"I didn't say anything. I was surprised and kind of happy that she didn't mind."

"That was a test." Fiona sighed.

"A test?"

"To see if you would have your head in the game. If you could be relied upon to stay focused. Maybe to see if I would be a distraction. Or if you would hold your tongue." Fiona could never really know what her grandmother thought about her relationships. But given how closely Leo was working with Grace, Fiona didn't trust her grandmother's magnanimous gesture.

Leo didn't look happy with the revelation. "I hate games."

"Not my thing, either. We can stop this, right now."

Leo tilted up her chin. Those soft brown eyes kept direct contact with hers. He didn't blink. No smirk. No words, either. But he hadn't answered. Doubt crept in, slithering up her spine to take hold of her courage. If she didn't fight it off, shoving it back to the black hole, she would lose focus on who was important and what she wanted.

He kissed her, a tender brush across the lips. His tongue orchestrated her surrender, taking her higher and higher into a conscious plane of erotic yearning. Her moistened sex ached to be satisfied only by him. "That's my answer." His thumb pressed gently against her mouth.

She kissed the pad of his thumb without taking her eyes off him. Their gazes locked, she parted her lips and sucked in the digit. Her tongue stroked him, curling around and cupping his thumb.

The few inches of space that had drifted between them closed in a snap.

His thumb slipped out of her mouth and his tongue plunged in to fill the space. She yielded to him. Pleasure flowed through her like the effects of a drug, heightening her senses. Taste. Touch. Her mouth was tuned for his devotion.

Her eyes were closed; she preferred to let the emotions paint an erotic picture for her imagination. As he ravaged her, kissing her neck, sucking on her lobe, she inhaled his scent like an elixir that kept her floating, spinning, tumbling through every stage of her re-awakened sexual hunger. When she greedily clung to him, he eased away until he hovered over her mouth. Their breaths, inhaled and exhaled, between them. She wanted to cry out for him to continue.

"Is that answer enough for you?"

She nodded. Every part of her trembled, shaky as she descended from the peak of ecstasy to rejoin the mortals.

Chapter 5

As soon as the sun dispatched its first rays above the horizon, Leo stepped outside the house suited up for a jog. After slipping in his earbuds, he selected his mixed-genre playlist. The lyrics and music set the pace for the entire range of his workout. He started off slowly to wake up his muscles. Each footfall energized him, waking up his stamina for the five-mile run.

The difference between his morning jog at home versus here in Water Mill was he usually had a full night of sleep. Being rested counted when the muscles burned from fatigue. So far this morning, he was operating on four hours of restless sleep. Maybe if he could push himself to the limit, then by the end of the day, he wouldn't have to second-guess Grace's intentions. Maybe then he could sprawl out in the king-size canopy bed and sink into dreamless sleep.

And he also wouldn't think about Fiona. The mere thought of her had his senses on overdrive. Her invasion past his defenses happened so fast that his emotions hadn't stopped their spiral spin. Wanting her was never in question. But, after they parted ways, he knew then, and knew now, that he needed her.

But what he didn't need was for his mind to meander through the archives of his childhood memories. Talking about his youth with Fiona had been a first. He'd rationalized that he shouldn't reveal anything of his past because it wasn't necessary to what he'd become. The boy from the poor village was not the man he'd transformed into, the lawyer he was now. Keeping those lives separate was a survival tactic. Otherwise, the anger and loss, the failure and hopelessness, would be lifelong companions.

Why should he have survived? He'd searched for the answer, some reason for being ripped away from his mother's arms and carried along with the mud and debris to be dumped into a shallow cave carved into the mountainside. His brothers, who were stronger than him, were gone. And his little sister…he couldn't ever forget. Leo turned up his pace, pumping his arms hard.

As a boy, he'd run barefoot from house to house. Everyone was family or close enough to be pulled into the circle. The equatorial heat and humidity never drained him, unlike the tourists who stomped through the rugged terrain on their ecotours, taking photos of him as if he were part of the natural landscape. While everyone paid expensive tour fees to enter and walk through the rain forest, this was his playground, where the lush, thick forests gave way to the flat grassy savannas. The rush of the Amazon River was only a few miles away;

again, not an amazing spectacle to his child's eye but simply a watery form of amusement and potential danger. Every animal and insect imaginable lived with the village's human inhabitants. He'd learned from an early age through warnings, scoldings and real-life danger what he should fear. But that was his life in those days: home, school and playing outdoors in the sweltering heat.

When he landed in Massachusetts, months after his home disappeared in the mudslide, he thought that he'd awoken into a nightmare of sounds and giants. Traffic resembled a stampede of metal, and he was surrounded by incessant car horns and people of all colors, none of whom wore cheery smiles and had ready greetings for each other. Buildings soared as if to compensate for the loss of the forests. Instead of delivering the steady temperature and mix of wet and dry seasons he knew, weather here operated like an angry *bruxa* sending her spells to whip up extreme cold and extreme heat.

To survive school and to fit in, he slammed the door on the past. Here, in America, was his future. There was really no place on his back big enough to carry the load of his loss, yearning and memories. And as far as the present, he'd been successful in his effort.

He'd come to accept restraint, focus and discipline as complements of his ability to keep the door firmly closed. But cracks had formed once he'd met Fiona. He did his best to stay the course, to block out his past.

No matter how hard he resisted, opening his heart to Fiona awoke feelings, gave life to emotions that he hadn't known he still had and made him hope. Those cracks in his defense kept up their progress, creating an imminent threat of a breakdown. After Fiona closed the door and walked out of his life, the one thing she couldn't do was push all the feelings she'd stirred in him back in the bottle to be sealed. The last three years, he'd coped and learned to shut off the valve to his emotions again.

Working with the Meadows family and being close to Fiona, Leo couldn't deny a tiny bubble of panic. The trials this family would endure and experience over this grandchild could shake loose his defenses. With Fiona looking to pick up where she'd left off, she was coming at him with her brand of supercharged sexual energy. While there would be backtracking through old terrain, his current focus was all about his legal career. He planned to take a few pages from her philosophy on life and keep the heart and mind separately contained and out of reach. Once was enough for a woman, *this woman*, to render him weak, vulnerable and emotionally out of control.

Leo's lungs burned for oxygen. The steep slope in the landscape had to be conquered. Everything unanchored in his life had to be conquered. His hamstrings screamed as he took on the incline. Sweat rolled down his forehead, dripping into his eyes. The sting was welcomed.

Maybe a bit of pain could keep his thoughts straight. On the outside, Fiona had floated into his life, but he might have the situation under control. On the inside, his turmoil was a nightly visitor—a dream.

He'd dreamed about his little sister, grinning up at him, showing off her missing front tooth. He had been the last one in the family to be shown her milestone. And it was the last time he'd seen her that day.

Sweat, tears—it didn't matter as they dripped down

his face. The uneven terrain was hell on his legs. Jogging to the brink of exhaustion was therapeutic, though. Otherwise, the ever-present ache for his family rendered him unmotivated to do anything. Hard to trust or believe in a happy-ever-after when in a flash every one he cherished had been ripped from his life. But this was his pain to bear. He kept it tucked close as he punished his body with his brutal exercise regimen.

Staying with the large Meadows family poked at the wound. Despite their drama, they proved repeatedly that they were unified and a protective force for each other. More than anything, his weakness had to remain undercover, preferably out of sight. Normally he'd function without any issues, without any nagging dreams. But Fiona ignited deep feelings within him, turning on the light in the darkest areas of his emotions. He pumped his arms to match the ramped-up speed of his jogging. Would be nice if he could outrun it all.

By the time Leo returned to the guesthouse, his legs suffered the shakes like a Jell-O mold. Water quenched his thirst and resuscitated his energy. Before he hopped into the shower, he called his sponsors—the only people who were close to being his family.

"Leo, good to hear from you." Freida still had strains of her German accent.

"How are you doing? And Franz?"

"Good. Good. Franz is back in Brazil. You know that is like his second home. I'm here catching up on a few things." She coughed.

"Are you sick?" To him, Freida was a boulder of good health and lots of cheer. She didn't believe in moping around and always wore a smile that could lift a dour mood in an instant.

"A little tickle in the throat. I'm a hearty German. Don't worry about me." They shared a laugh because German blood was the reason for anything good and strong in her life. "It really is good to hear from you. Fill me in on what you're up to."

He did. Since he'd left Massachusetts, he didn't call often. Most times, Freida and Franz were working with the same charity in some country or other, helping native populations to survive and cope after disasters. He'd finally encouraged them to use email, which hid any of the awkwardness he showed during their live interactions.

"Franz is in São Miguel village. Your childhood home," she prompted when he didn't react. "He's still looking, Leo."

"Thanks." Leo gripped the phone, fighting the urge to toss it to the floor. Although he didn't have the courage to go back, Franz made an annual pilgrimage to look for any of his relatives. Every year, he returned with no developments. After a while, Leo wished that he'd stop. The continued hope and disappointment crushed his soul.

"I'll tell him that you called."

"Yeah." His emotion choked off further speech.

"Be safe. Continue to make us proud. Bye, Leo."

Leo hung up and stayed immobile. No sense in his getting emotional over Franz's doggedness. There was nothing back in São Miguel.

Life happened—the good and the not so good.

He clenched his jaw and exhaled. Only then did he move and head for the shower.

He blasted his body first with frigid water, then as hot as his skin could bear. He needed to clear away the sweat and dirt of his run. But he also needed to break free from his mind and his own nagging demons, even if temporarily. Skipping the breakfast fare at the main house, he opted to be in his own space for a little while longer. He made breakfast from the fruit that he'd bought at the open-air market. Keeping an eye on the time, he enjoyed his meal while catching up on work emails.

Done with everything, he declared, "Time to deal with the Meadowses."

He headed up the garden path, now that he was aware of the shortcut that would take him through the garage and into the house. He passed and greeted the various house staff. As he walked past the windows, he could see someone was taking an early-morning swim in the pool. The house was stirring to life. He picked up his pace, wanting to be early for his meeting with Grace.

After a few wrong twists and turns, he walked into the open hallway and past the grand staircase. He instinctively looked up to see if Fiona might be coming down the steps. Luck wasn't on his side. The sleepy quietness on the second floor was in contrast to the gradual busyness on the first floor. Why not? They were on vacation.

"Ah, Leo, good to see you early for the meeting." Grace appeared ahead of him from one of the many rooms.

"Yep, I'm ready to get to work."

"Good. I like a healthy work ethic."

They bantered until they walked into her office. Then the doors closed and the atmosphere changed from casual, friendly, attentive interest in each other's comfort to a solemn, intense all-business approach.

Grace took her seat behind the desk, making it clear where he needed to be seated. The other option was on the right side of her large executive desk.

Against the windows overlooking the back of the house, the large office contained two other sitting areas for bigger group discussions. One space was furnished with a small conference table to seat six and the other had a thick leather couch and two single chairs. The remaining wall space was lined with bookshelves and decorations that weren't of the Ikea variety.

While she prepared her desk for their meeting, he sat opposite her waiting for the day's instructions. Yesterday they'd shared time over breakfast. Today they were working together on the Meadows family.

He took the plunge and started. "I have contracted an investigator who solely handles finding adopted children."

"Good." She peered over her reading glasses. Her mouth scrunched as she waited for him to continue.

"No disrespect, but you could have done that."

"I could have." She pursed her lips but then cleared her throat with a slight cough. "I thought you the best person for the job. While you are bound by legal ethics, I also needed someone who could empathize with the various angles of the delicate situation."

Seconds ticked by before Leo fully understood Grace's explanation. "You've checked into my background."

"Naturally. You are handling my affairs. I wouldn't let just anyone into my house."

"Oh."

"No one knows," she offered, with that surprising gentleness that could melt ice off a cold heart.

Finally, he said, "The adoption wasn't closed." What else was there to say?

"Then my daughter has known where he was all this time?" The reading glasses were taken off and dangled between her manicured fingers.

"Not necessarily. It only means that it shouldn't be too difficult to find him." Leo hoped.

Grace seemed to take what he said and digest it. With a quick nod, she motioned with her hand. "Now for the will." The reading glasses slid back into place.

"We don't know if he'd be amenable to your gifts." Leo wanted to slow down her blind faith that this scenario would be an easy family reunion.

"I understand. But I could have a heart attack like this…" She snapped her fingers. "And then nothing will have been in place."

Leo, of all people, easily acknowledged that everyone on earth would die. But in Grace's case, he felt that her iron tenacity would be her bargaining chip to get things her way before she went to the other side.

He arranged the major portions of the will along her desk. He had no idea if she was revamping every piece or one of the categories of her assets.

She read through some of the paperwork. "I also want to amend the trust. I want to work with an orphanage."

Every detail, every wish was noted. Eventually, he'd have to bring in the president of the family trust to fine-tune the details. Until the grandson was found, he had to operate like a one-person multioperational unit. For now, he went along with the program. Although he knew that it wasn't the most effective or efficient way to accomplish the tasks. He wondered why Grace, praised for her efficient business acumen, wanted to work like this. Privacy didn't seem to be reason enough, when a full legal team would be held to the same ethical standards and be quicker.

But his success would bring him a significant career boost. A recommendation from Grace could fast-forward the momentum of his professional path, and one piece of caustic feedback from her could tear the foundation from under his career aspirations.

A knock on the door interrupted their discussion. Grace bade entry. The door opened slowly before Fiona popped in her head. Her face was tense. She didn't look in his direction. Her grandmother waved her into the room.

Leo straightened up. His body went on alert at Fiona's distress. He almost jumped up to ask her what the matter was.

"Mom said she's leaving. Today. Right now." Her agitation rose with every word.

"What?" Grace might be pushing the eighty-year mark, but she still had an agility that surprised everyone. She was around her desk and at the door in seconds. "She can't leave."

"Speak to her, Grandma," Fiona pleaded, following her to the door. "Please."

Leo heard the pain, although the visual was even stronger. Fiona wasn't the type to get emotional and chatty about her feelings. That was why seeing her clutch her grandmother's arm, her expression sad but her tone hopeful for Grace's help, had him walking toward them.

He had every intention to reassure her, while holding her against his chest, that everything would be all right. He stopped just shy of them. That would be the normal reaction if they were a couple.

Common sense intervened. Grace was providing the emotional strength that he wanted to, but couldn't, offer to her granddaughter. All he could do was hover on the sideline. Once Grace went to find Verona, he didn't know whether to go to Fiona or give her space and return to the desk. He didn't know how to comfort her, because he didn't know why she was upset.

The clock's ticking and Fiona's sighs punctuated the quietness of the large room. She remained at the door, gripping the handle. She hadn't acknowledged him. Giving her space was more important. He resettled in the chair.

His adjustment snagged her attention. She looked over at him, as if noticing his presence for the first time. The furrowed brow and worry-laced gaze melted away into the tight set of her face and arms as she gave a frosty glare. It didn't take long for her to move from the door and plant herself in front of him.

"Are you okay?" he asked, seeing the answer but wanting to be the first to speak.

"What the hell is going on?"

"What?" Leo slowly pushed himself out of the chair. The hints were loud and brash that this conversation wouldn't be one filled with tender quips.

"Why is my family acting weirder than normal? My mother, who could be a clone to Grace, looked on the verge of an emotional collapse. I couldn't talk to her. My father couldn't talk to her. Something's up."

Her eyes added an exclamation point with their direct blast on him.

"And you blame me for your mother's departure?"

"Yes!" She stomped her foot. "No."

He would have much rather she'd been as emphatic with her *no*. But he'd take what he could get.

"You don't have to tell me the details, but is what you're working on with Grace…going to affect my mother?"

"No." The lie came so easily that Leo paused to weigh the serious step he'd just taken. He truly didn't know what else to say. *Not at liberty to say* would have been so much better. But he wanted her to stop worrying, stop being suspicious of her mother, stop all the questioning leveled at him. And so he took a dangerous road that he knew would have consequences, even if it meant that his guilt tore at his gut.

"Working for my grandmother might not be worth it in the end." She shifted her gaze to the paperwork of the will still laid out on the desk. "I really hope you know what you're doing," she fired at him. Her eyes glistened with unshed tears.

"I know that I am capable of doing my job. Addressing my client's requests." Leo fought to sound even-keeled. "And I know that your grandmother has everyone's best interests at heart."

"Pat me on my head and tell me it's the adults in charge."

"No. Not all. It's—"

She spun away from him and headed around the desk. Her eyes were laser focused on the paperwork.

But he reached out, grabbing her arm to stop her. "Don't. Don't lose faith in Grace." He wanted to say *in him*. But she'd never had faith in him. She hadn't thought him up to par, equal with her, when she explained why they were better off apart than together. "Be patient," he finished.

Under the grip of his fingers, he felt the tension leave her body.

As if it was the most natural thing to do, he gently drew her into his arms. Her body yielded against his and he held her as she rested her head against his shoulder. Her hair brushed his chin.

"I want the uneasy feeling to go away," she said with a sigh.

"There's nothing to make you worry. You're surrounded by good people."

She leaned away, but not out of his arms. "And you're one of the good people?" Her smile erased any bite.

"I'm on the team of the best people," he bragged.

Before she could say anything, he kissed her. There was no demand in his touch. Nor did he crave anything beyond offering comfort. Though she hadn't a clue about the goings-on, he wanted her to know that he was there for her.

His lips and hers formed the perfect seal.

Leo hadn't known much about the Meadows family when he dated Fiona. Her entry into his life was like a sudden hurricane that crashed through, uprooting his expectations about love.

"I agree with your assessment," she said after their brief kiss. "Don't change that. Don't turn it off. Not even for Grace."

Her kind remarks touched his core, leaving him with a warm glow.

Grace reentered with Verona in tow. By then, he and Fiona, no longer in each other's arms, watched their march into the room. Verona looked reluctant and very startled when she noticed Fiona's presence. Leo took a casual step closer to Fiona. Their shoulder-to-shoulder stance could hardly be considered a united front. Fiona's body, like his, grew tense, readying for the play-out of the situation.

"Fiona, would you excuse us, please?" Grace's dismissal carried no edge.

However, Fiona didn't budge. Instead she looked at her mother—waiting for her input, perhaps?

"I won't talk while she's here." Verona barely looked at Fiona and pointedly kept her eyes on Grace.

"I'm your daughter." Fiona looked at Grace for help. "Maybe I should be here. Need to be here." Her plea ended with the back of her hand furtively brushing against Leo's. An impromptu partnership for the skirmish ahead.

Grace raised her hand to put a halt to Fiona's stand. "Not yet, dear."

"Not ever," Verona snapped. "Oh, Mother, you can-*not* do this."

Leo shifted his weight, uneasy with this detour from business meeting into a moment ripe for a family counseling session. His hand no longer touched Fiona's, because she'd stepped away at her mother's less-than-welcoming outburst.

"Fiona—"

"Grandma, don't bother. I'll leave the secret talks for the inner circle. And someday, Mom, you should stop thinking that everything is all about you. I'm not an inconvenience." Fiona stormed out of the office, slamming the door behind her.

Leo rocked up on his toes and settled back into his stance. Fiona's fiery delivery was epic. He buried the inappropriate chuckle attempting to erupt from the base of his throat. The effort wasn't completely successful. Verona directed her cold scrutiny over his entire body. *Damn.*

"Why is he here?" Verona asked. Her scowl seemed to be a permanent feature.

"Leo is assisting me with finding my grandchild."

"You told me he was working on the will." Verona's attention snapped back to Grace. The revelation turned up her displeasure a notch.

"That, too."

Maybe Grace knew how to handle her eldest daughter. He was impressed with the soothing calmness of her voice, as if all of this—whatever *this* was—had a reasonable explanation. His management of irate clients didn't extend to mothers who felt threatened and betrayed by family members.

"You are determined to go through with this." Verona kept him in her sight as she addressed Grace. "How could you?"

"Ever since you told me the news of my grandson, I have blamed myself for not knowing. Your stay at college was no excuse for not telling me. Looks like I wasn't the mother who you could confide in with such a tremendous burden but also a tremendous blessing. But when you reach my age, when tomorrow isn't guaranteed, wisdom has a way of sinking in. What's important has a way of knocking on stubborn heads—like mine. I don't have time to sit around surrounded by

regrets. At my eightieth birthday, I want my family—
everyone—there to celebrate with me." Now Grace sat
in the chair Leo had vacated, not behind the desk where
she normally sat to oversee her business and family
matters. Instead she was a mother talking to her child.

Leo didn't doubt Grace's sincerity. Although he was
shocked that she spoke so plainly and honestly in front
of him. But neither woman paid him any mind. From
his viewpoint, he was the spectator at a private show.

Grace displayed her shrewdness in assuming the
role of peacekeeper whose actions were misunderstood.
No public interview he'd ever seen had captured the
inner feelings of this powerful woman.

But she wasn't done, as she continued, "Why didn't
you tell me, Verona? You knew that once you'd told
me, I would want to meet this young man. For almost
thirty-five years, this life has grown without my love."
She paused and uttered a dry chuckle. "Some might
argue that's a good thing."

Verona hung her head. Despite the sophisticated tailored pantsuit, sensible heels and no-nonsense bun she
wore, she looked like the young, college-aged mother-
to-be she had been who was afraid of so much. "You'll
continue on with or without me."

"Yes."

Verona stared at the floor.

"But I'd rather have you as an ally."

Her daughter's head shot up. "And thus the Meadows empire was born."

"And lasted." Grace's tone was unapologetic.

"Then I don't have to stay."

As the vested observer, Leo knew what he wanted
out of this dilemma—to give Grace her grandson and

to give Verona some peace of mind. But for Fiona, he wanted to rebuild what they had torn down between them. He wanted to see her and her mother reconcile and the rocky road between her and Grace smoothed over.

Maybe everything he wanted was too much to hope for, considering that his secret—his role—would cause her pain. His actions might be seen as such a betrayal that he wouldn't be able to fix it with hug and a kiss.

He stepped up squarely into the spotlight. "Verona, if I may, would you at least consider staying until I've completed my investigation? You might change your mind."

A slow turn of her head, and she said, "You don't get to weigh in on this."

"I beg to differ. Leo's assistance is exemplary. I would rather not have a fight among the family and with my guest. So please reconsider leaving today. You could help us."

Verona turned her shoulders away from him. "No, I certainly will not help you with this, as if it's some weepy cable movie. But I will wait for his report." At least she'd acknowledged that he had an important role.

"Then go to Fiona and make peace with your daughter," Grace urged with less softness and more firmness.

Verona didn't indicate that she agreed to Grace's last request or that she'd do it. Instead she left the room without another word, taking along with her the snap-and-crackle vibes that had killed the earlier workflow.

"With all due respect, Grace, I feel that this would go a lot easier if you and Verona moved with one accord," Leo said.

"With all due respect, Leo, we did start out with one

accord to find the child. Verona has waffled. I have not. She will come round." Her final sentiment didn't have the usual hubris.

"Yes, ma'am." He opened his notebook. "Then let's back to work."

She rewarded him with a wide smile. "Good work ethic. You continue to impress me."

Leo held on to the compliment. He was getting good at pretending. No one suspected the battle waged between his conscience and with heart.

Fiona fumed. She didn't like being tossed out of Grace's office. She certainly didn't like being ignored by her mother. And as for Leo, well... She paused to consider his offense—not stepping up to her defense. But was that a crime? "He's definitely working for Grace. Probably could be employee of the week," she mused aloud.

"A good thing, right?" Belinda playfully pulled on Fiona's hair.

Fiona smiled. "Yeah. I guess."

"Oh, well, that sounds like a promising, juicy bit." Belinda waited for her to continue.

"Well, kinda..." Fiona sighed and left her cousin hanging. Instead she switched gears away from the very personal tidbits. As she sat on the bedroom window seat of her favorite lookout point over the front driveway, she remarked, "What could they possibly be talking about that has my mother acting like a ditz?"

"It's not like you aren't all melodramatic." Dana blew on her fingers after painting her nails neon green. She sat cross-legged on Fiona's bed. "I'm really liking this vacation. I feel...liberated."

"Whatever that means." Belinda walked to the other window seat.

"I'm feeling unburdened. No phones. No meetings," Dana went on to explain between puffs of breath over her wet nails.

"Who are you kidding?" Belinda interrupted. "I could see the bedroom light was still on from under the door for most of the night. You're still working."

"I could be talking to Kent." Dana made a face.

"Yeah, you could. But we all know that the CEO position doesn't allow a complete shutdown. The job is like the offspring that never grows up and never goes away." Belinda offered the bleak version of Dana's accomplishment.

"Excuse me, but I'm the one with the issues." Fiona didn't want to hear the battle of who got the best deal, between working for Meadows or striking out on her own. It was a no-win debate and they both knew it. Dana's passion was born and bred at Meadows Media. Belinda's passion came out of a terrible accident. In Fiona's estimation, they had both lucked out with following their hearts.

"Sorry, Fiona. Did you ever think that maybe Grace is sick?" Belinda said softly, as if the very suggestion was taboo.

"Or maybe my mother?" Fiona wondered if that was why Verona looked as if she was barely holding on, as if any one thing could trigger a blowup.

"I say we bum-rush Grandpa." Dana clapped her hands, still careful with the nails.

Belinda chimed in, "Now, that sounds like a plan. When and where?"

"Let's kidnap him and take him into town. Tomorrow at ten. Grace will be with Leo." Fiona was down for a little guerrilla warfare.

"All in?" Dana asked.

"Always," Belinda and Fiona responded together.

From below, under Fiona's window, voices wafted up to her lookout point. She signaled to her cousins to stop talking. They hurried over to her spot and huddled around her to see and hear what was going on.

Fiona whispered, with her forehead pressed against the window, "It's my mother."

"Ours, too. They're all huddled together." Belinda joined her with her forehead also smashed against the glass.

"Open this window." Dana's frustration matched Fiona's.

Fiona fiddled with the stubborn window latch. "Damn, it's stuck. I can't hear what they're saying."

"Oh, wait…they're hugging. Good grief, are they crying? I haven't seen our mothers do anything together in years." For the first time, Belinda sounded worried.

"They are getting into Aunt Verona's car," Dana announced, as if they couldn't see the activity.

"Wait." Fiona shifted to kneeling on the window seat. "Leo just left. He's walking toward the guesthouse."

"Yeah, but I think your mother may run him down first." Dana snorted.

Fiona pushed aside her cousins and hightailed it out of her room. Not until she was halfway down the stairs did she notice her bare feet. But she wasn't about to waste time running back up to get her sandals. She had a bigger mission. Saving Leo from her mother.

Her feet hit the marbled floor and she didn't slow down until she yanked open the front door. Her mother's car had pulled up alongside Leo. From Verona's expression, Fiona was sure that the one-sided conversation wasn't her mother being complimentary.

"Leo. Oh, good—glad that I didn't miss you for lunch." She stepped in and hooked her hand through his arm.

He looked at her and then down at her feet.

"I'm hungry. Are you going to fix me that meal you promised? Now?" Fiona ignored the sharp pebbles digging into her feet.

"Um…that was going to be a dinner invite." He looked uncomfortable with the riveted audience in the car.

"Lunch. Dinner. Doesn't matter." While her intent had been to rescue him from her mother's wrath, she was sounding desperate.

"Verona, let's go. We'll miss our reservation." Belinda's mother waved at them. Elaine tossed them an apologetic smile, while Verona drove off without changing her expression of distaste at Leo. Fiona didn't exhale until the car disappeared down the driveway.

"Well, aren't you just the bohemian? Nice change." Leo's chuckle had her smiling.

Fiona removed her hand from his arm. "Yes, well. Figured you shouldn't get your head ripped off by my mother or aunts as I watch." Fiona turned to head back into the house.

"Does this mean that, now they're gone, I have to eat alone?"

"I'm sure lunch is about to be served here." She

gestured with her thumb at the house. "I don't want to force you into feeding me."

"Force me? I'd be happy to feed you and watch you eat. I've got mad cooking skills. And if it isn't good enough, I'm sure Mrs. Finch will take care of my deficiencies with a meal upon your request."

"Don't have to invite me twice. Okay, let's go." The first step had Fiona wincing. The second step, Fiona howled.

"I'll wait for you to get your shoes." He shook his head at her wounded feet.

"Stop fussing. I can do this and walk to the guesthouse."

"A country girl, you are not." He squatted in front of her. "Hop on. You weigh as much as a twig anyway. Let's go, Lula Mae, the wannabe country girl."

Fiona couldn't believe she was doing this, but that didn't stop her from climbing onto Leo's back. Once settled, she wrapped her arms loosely around his neck. His arms easily supported her legs before he rose with her in one fluid movement.

A dull cheer from above let her know that her cousins had witnessed the entire minidrama.

Chapter 6

Fiona walked with Leo, or more accurately, he carried her to the guesthouse. Although she might not be the weight of a truck, she knew it was laborious to walk on the graveled driveway in dress clothes with her body sealed against his back. She'd save her conversations for when they were at his house. Maybe she'd be coherent after the sensations now present in her sex, which was pressed and rubbing against Leo's back, subsided after the exquisite stimulation.

He unknowingly stretched out the torture by not lowering her to solid ground until he took her into the living room. Then she slid off, aroused and barely in control enough to stand, and had to pretend nothing extraordinary was going on all over her body and especially between her legs.

"Water, wine, beer…?" He ambled to the kitchen.

"You're quite stocked."

"Most of this was here. Mrs. Finch gave me the green light to use whatever I wanted."

"I'll take water." Fiona was parched.

He poured a glass of water from a filtered pitcher and handed it to her. She gratefully accepted it to soothe her dry throat. The only part of her body that was soothed.

"Take a seat at the counter. I'll fix you a delicious peanut butter and jelly sandwich," he said.

"Yummy."

"And it looks as if Mrs. Finch dropped off a freshly baked loaf of apple-cinnamon bread and a pan of brownies."

"The brownies win and they smell divine. How about we start with them?"

"Nope. No desserts before the meal." He pulled the pan out of reach. "Go wash up. Bathroom is that way." He laughed. "Oh yeah, you already know the layout."

Fiona headed to the bathroom, but she was also planning to peek into the bedroom as she walked past it. She paused in the doorway. Everything was neat and in its place. Nothing there had changed. He was neat. She wasn't.

She stood at the sink, looking at her reflection. Maybe she should have put on a touch of makeup. She scrutinized every angle of her face, noticing all the imperfections. After washing her hands and drying them, she fluffed out her hair. That was about all she could do to feel pretty.

By the time she'd returned to the kitchen, the sandwich was ready with a diagonal cut separating the two halves.

"Potato chips or cheese curls?" He pointed to the goodies.

"I'll take the chips. Please don't tell me that you're not eating."

"Made myself a protein shake." He held up his glass of thick liquid.

"You already look fine. All that major jogging is unnecessary."

"You saw me jogging this morning?"

She shrugged. *Busted.*

"I have to look my best."

"For whom?" Fiona didn't care if she sounded possessive.

"Any eligible bachelorettes out there."

Fiona choked on her sandwich. "Were there many of these eligible...?"

He nodded, then sipped on his concoction.

"Liar!" For a second, jealousy hit her in the chest. Its claws squeezed the air out of her lungs. But he'd never been the type to string along the ladies. She had to admit, however, that he'd aged well, filled out the muscles, and he still kissed like a badass rock star. Was he now sexy-nerd-turned-playboy?

"Do you want me to name them all?"

She sipped her water, looking at him over the rim. Time to weigh his guilt or innocence. She'd done her fair share of interrogations. "Go on, amuse me. Alphabetical order."

He grinned. "Aubergine. Berry. Cauli. Dasheen."

"Hold up. Cauli?" Fiona laughed and kept eating. "I almost got jealous."

"Almost?"

"See, you didn't think that I know my fruits and veggies. Cauli, indeed." She snorted.

"Now I feel you're making fun of my women."

"My bad. So Cauli gave you what you needed?"

"And then some." He tipped his head back and finished his drink, smacking his lips.

"That would be a shame if you were hooked only on veggies."

"Cauliflower was good for my soul."

She leaned forward and kissed him. "No, she wasn't. I was." She kissed him again. "I still am."

"Is this a hostile takeover?"

"You betcha." She pulled off her shirt and tossed it aside. "How long is your lunch break?"

"Long enough." He hadn't moved from around the counter. "That is, if I wasn't planning on a lunchtime diversion."

Her shorts were off her hips when she paused. "Sounds like your problem. I'm initiating the acquisition of your assets. Is that lawyer-speak enough for you?" She stepped out of her shorts and stood in place in her bra and panties.

"I feel like I need a safe word."

"If that makes you feel safe with me." She unhooked her bra and tossed it on the heap of clothes. "I'll be gentle."

Hurriedly, he set the dishes on the counter behind him. Then he motioned for her to come closer. Not waiting an extra second, Fiona climbed onto the counter and knelt in front of him. She reached up for the pot rack to stabilize her position.

"I think that I'm definitely ready to put the vegetables aside. You are my dessert—a mouthwatering brownie." He looked up at her.

"A wise man said that you shouldn't eat your desserts before the meal."

"What the hell does he know?"

She flipped her legs over the side to sit facing him before sliding them open for him. He didn't hesitate to plant himself between her legs, with his hands resting on her thighs. No set game plan existed to guide what would come next. Why bother thinking ahead? Fiona wanted to go with the flow.

Thankfully, so did Leo. His hands now gripped the edge of the counter. His shoulders hunched as he lowered his body so that their faces lined up. Fiona squirmed against the hard surface of the counter. She was ready to melt into a puddle. His steady gaze heated her, as if she were standing under the fierce rays of the sun.

He leaned in and kissed her softly on her lips before pulling back to look at her. Those brown eyes bathed her skin with the promise of another scorching kiss. This time she arched her neck to offer the sensitive skin for his lips to land on.

First his lips branded her. Then his tongue brushed her skin, almost sending her into a convulsion. Cries of pleasure curled up and out from a place deep inside. With her grip on the counter, she was poised to dive into the deep end.

Once she took the plunge, she sank under the waves in bliss. His hand cupped her breast, guiding her pert nipple to his mouth. Her breath hissed hard between clenched teeth. A shock rippled through her system. Each time his teeth grazed the sensitive bud, her hips bucked on the counter. *Oh, sweet torture.* The sensual assault expanded to the other breast. A punishment that she desperately wanted to never end.

He pulled off her panties. "You won't be needing those."

"Good to know."

He obliged with soft kisses peppered in a straight line down to her belly button. Gently, he pulled her hips forward to meet his ready tongue—a gentle swipe to her clit.

Her mind short-circuited.

Her body heated.

Her sex pulsed.

He pressed an erotic kiss to the tender lips between her legs. Fiona gasped. For a second, she scrambled to breathe as his tongue assaulted her in the sweetest way. Her eyes squeezed shut so she could mentally focus on every tiny detail of the ride.

"I want you to come for me, Fiona."

Fiona gasped. "Make me."

His answering smile promised wicked fun. When his finger slipped into her wet cave, she just about lost it. Each stroke was a slow, deep slide back and forth against her walls. Slick and ready, she wanted all of him.

But he was done playing fair, double-teaming with his tongue and finger.

"You're beautiful, inside and out. Top to bottom." He pressed his lips to her clit and pulled her between his lips. Once he got going, there was no stopping.

Her hands reached out to grasp something, anything. She had only the smooth surface of the counter, where her nails raked over the top.

Her hips rose, egging him on. Urging him in. She couldn't wait any longer.

He unfastened his pants and slipped on a condom, and his hands closed possessively over her hips.

His arousal pointed toward her opening. Yet he didn't make a move.

"Are you going to make me beg?" She was ready to, if necessary.

"No. I like it when you are bossy and ready to kick ass." He grabbed her. "Hold on."

He was sexy as hell when he lifted her with one hand around her body. He walked to the bedroom and kicked open the door. "You ready to take it home?"

"All the way…right now!"

He gently laid her on the bed. But she wasn't going to let him get away. No more talking. No more dawdling.

She pulled him on her, in her.

They rode the wave together. Holding on to each other. Staring into each other's eyes. Their bodies spoke a language that needed no words. They fed off the energy. Tasting the sweet fruit of their seduction. In each other's arms, they stayed locked in an embrace.

She rocked against his thrusts, opening herself to him.

Then he released, acting like a trigger for her.

Fiona could compare the moment only to shock waves after an earthquake. She held on for dear life, riding the pulsing rhythms that kept on coming. There was no rushing the moment. She let go and let her body have its celebration.

"I think I missed my postlunch check-in time with

Grace." His voice was muffled in her hair, where his head rested.

"If you want me to write a note, I'd be willing." Fiona laughed, slightly giddy that she was now in Leo's arms after a midday delight. A fantasy turned reality. This wonderful moment wasn't about winning. She didn't want to conquer this gorgeous man who took her to the brink of sanity with his lovemaking. Instead, she wanted to be invited in to the innermost region of his heart and offered to stay a while. She sighed. She hoped for that fantasy to turn into reality.

The daily routine for the week didn't deviate much for Leo. Early-morning jog, then a meeting with Grace, followed by hot sex with Fiona, more work with Grace and dinner with the family. Occasionally, he'd spend the late evening with Fiona, but family time intervened and the cousins would scoop her up for their ladies-only diversions. The situation was clear: hot sex and postcoital cuddling and chatting were the primary activities of their relationship. That shouldn't be a bad thing. Yet he found himself managing a growing disappointment. He wanted more, even as he felt the addiction for her hit the point of no return.

With the onset of the weekend, he had a lot of time on his hands. He wasn't going to ask Fiona on an official date and he wasn't going to sit around pining for her time. He'd done that during their first go-round as the naïve one falling hard and heavy with disastrous results. That was why he eagerly jumped at Jesse's invitation to hang with him and Kent, who had arrived midweek.

"Where are we headed?" Leo asked after he got into the car and greeted the guys.

"We're going to look at real estate," Kent said.

"Cool." He'd been hoping they weren't going to say hiking or canoeing. He couldn't take more rigorous activity. His legs were still sore from the extra mile that he'd tacked on to his workout and his body overall was still recovering from the vigorous rounds of lovemaking.

"And why are you looking for real estate?" Jesse asked. "Planning for the long term?"

"I like it out here. Ever since my move from England, I've been balancing my time between business and tourist traps," Kent explained.

"You've barely been here," Jesse teased. Clearly, the two were close friends.

"I came out here one weekend when Grace was staying at the estate. At the time, I'd been hired to coach Dana for the CEO position."

"That must have been tough. Not the coaching part, but dealing with Grace and handing things over to the next generation."

Leo paid attention to their conversation, recognizing themes applicable to his situation.

Kent answered, "Was a bit bumpy, but Dana proved she could take on the business. Had to get Grace to give her the space and room to breathe."

"She didn't mind you dating her granddaughter?" Leo jumped in.

"I'm sure she was concerned, but I had to prove myself, too." Kent paused and looked directly at Leo through the rearview mirror. "I did."

"Are you taking notes?" Jesse asked over his shoulder.

"Me?" Leo realized that he'd just opened the door to his personal goings-on.

"Yes, you. Don't try to play the innocent. We all know that you and Fiona have your special thing. You'd have to be on another planet not to see the vibes."

"And you must be damn good at what you do for Grace because you're still here." Jesse gave him a thumbs-up.

The gesture didn't do much for Leo's worries about Grace and the special assignment, and Grace and her eldest granddaughter. Over and over again, he heard the same standard for a good job—Grace's approval. She was his reality and, in a way, his path to career happiness. At least, that was what he'd thought of as the absolute truth before coming to the Hamptons.

Now his heart and mind were in sync with the uncomfortable revelation that solely focusing on the career didn't satisfy any part of him. He needed more out of life for that special brand of happiness. His search didn't have to be extensive. The solution, his woman, could be a part of his life, if he didn't screw it up.

"Here we are." Kent pulled up in front of a massive house that looked like a baby mansion. He turned off the engine.

"Whoa!" Jesse exclaimed before Leo voiced his amazement. "I thought you meant a little country cottage."

"You're buying this?" Leo gazed at the property, but it was too massive for an all-in-one view. He had to take the expansive front scene in sections. Each visual portion could have been its own house. "Why?"

His question hung in between Jesse's continued colorful exclamations.

Kent was quiet, reflective, as he stood outside the car with arms folded in front of the electronic gate.

"Tell me again, what is this house going to be?" Jesse asked.

"This is my wedding gift to Dana. I'll propose at Grace's birthday. Permission has been granted."

"Whoa!" Jesse seemed stuck in his awe. "You are going to set the bar too high in the sky for us. I was going to get Belinda a horse."

Kent and Leo laughed.

"No, really. We're blowing up with the business. Potential clients are on a wait list. For Christmas I am getting her another horse. Will tie a nice red bow to its mane. I'm going to have a sash made that says 'Merry Christmas, Belinda. I love you.'"

Kent and Jesse looked expectantly at Leo.

Leo raised his hands in surrender. "Don't look at me. I can barely think about tomorrow, much less Christmas. But a horse from you and a house—let's call it what it is, a mansion—from you is a bit much for me to compete with. I got nothing on y'all."

"So what do you think?" Kent turned to Leo.

"I'd say Dana is lucky to have a thoughtful guy."

Kent shook Leo's shoulders. "I know you want to choke her."

"Just a smidgen." Leo patted Kent's back. "This will be awesome."

"So are you in for the groomsmen? I'm talking to both of you." Kent offered his question to both men.

"Yeah," Jesse exclaimed.

"Sure." Leo replied, with more than a slice of doubt that he'd still be in Fiona's life.

Not that he wanted such a bleak finale. But time might not be on his side to establish himself as a strong anchor in Fiona's life. Listening to these men, who had pushed past their challenges to be with their women, did give him hope. Maybe he could learn a thing or two from them. He was ready for the lessons.

"Good. Let's look around and then get some food. Then I want to hear about you and Fiona." Kent threw his arms around them and walked down the hallway, which was wide enough for the three of them to walk side by side with room to spare.

"Definitely want to hear how fast you fell under the spell of love." Jesse slapped his back.

"Naw…" Leo protested easily, as if it was what he should do.

"Don't bother to deny or defend." Jesse shrugged. "It is what it is."

"We've been where you are. My advice—don't waste time pondering." Kent detached himself from the group and walked ahead. "Now, let me show you the rest of the house."

Leo had to admit to the sense of relief that washed over him. To be pulled into the circle by these guys meant a lot. They were members of a unique fraternity.

Fiona lounged at the pool, sipping her lemonade. She'd already done a couple laps and now wanted to relax before jumping in for another dip. The guys hadn't returned yet. Although she knew where they'd gone, she was still curious as to how they were getting along. Part of her was desperate for Leo to fit in and for the family to like him. So far, even if they hadn't quite warmed to him, they didn't hate him... Well, maybe only her mother.

Belinda stepped in, blocking her contact with the sunshine. With a mischievous smile, her cousin leaned over and squeezed the water from her hair. Fiona squealed and pulled up her legs from the cool splatter of water.

Belinda took a long drink of Fiona's lemonade. "Ah...that's good."

"Go away." Fiona laughed at her outrageous behavior.

Belinda got comfortable in the chair next to Fiona's. "Just about seven days gone, so...how are things with you and lover boy?"

"Fantastic." Fiona couldn't help gushing. "It's like the second time around is sweeter."

"I'm not trying to find out."

"I know... No one wants to think about breaking up."

"Do you regret breaking up with him? If it was so wrong then, do you think that it's better now?"

Fiona shrugged. "We're older. That helps." She'd pondered those questions and couldn't admit that she didn't have a clear answer. "He was young. Fresh out of university. First major internship. He didn't need me holding him back. His life was ahead of him."

"I think you got scared of people gossiping that you were his sugar mama."

Fiona groaned. "I hate that name."

"But you weren't. He had a *J-O-B*. You let people get into your head." Belinda smiled and nudged her leg with hers. "Have to say that the few years haven't been bad on him, either. Brazil is offering up some mighty fine exports, if you ask me."

"And no one is asking you." Fiona didn't need Belinda's confirmation that Leo was looking finer than ever.

"Hell, I could be a broker for brides."

"Girl, you'd better stick with your horses. Now, that's your gold touch in motion right there."

"It is, isn't it? I never thought that I'd be in heaven with my horses."

"Horses and children." Fiona could see her cousin's future.

Belinda nodded.

"What did I miss?" Dana stood between them as she dripped from her swim in the pool. "What did you say to her to make her teary?" Her gaze shifted from accusatory to concerned as it moved from Fiona to Belinda.

Fiona rolled her eyes. "Relax. She's happy about her horses."

Dana joined them, grabbing her chair to enjoy and soak up the sun. "When are the guys returning?"

"I don't know. But they volunteered to cook us barbecue. And I'm famished," Belinda groused.

Fiona's stomach growled at the mention of food.

"We heard that." Kent walked in with his arms loaded with bags.

"Baby, you're back." Dana jumped up from her chair and launched herself at Kent.

Belinda and Jesse weren't far behind with a big reunion hug, despite it having been four or five hours since they'd last seen the men.

Fiona stayed put. Jumping on Leo was reserved for their eyes only.

From his expression, she knew he was on the same page.

"We're hungry," Belinda complained. "Start the grill and we'll get changed."

"Deal," Kent responded. He and Dana kissed as though she were setting off on a long journey.

Belinda, at least, didn't go over the top and just waved to Jesse.

Fiona didn't run up to Leo but sauntered past in his line of sight. She'd deliberately worn her tiny red bikini for him. She delayed tying her sarong around her waist, giving him his own personal view of her behind before she covered it. She couldn't help throwing him a flirty glance over her shoulder. His answering wink told her that tonight he'd respond in a robust way to her sexy invite.

The barbecue cookout was a success, if Fiona had to give her public review of the fantastic meal. She couldn't eat another bite. Kent had outdone himself playing master chef at the grill. Steaks were juicy. The meat was tender and falling off the ribs. She'd passed on the bratwurst because her jeans would have ripped at the seams.

After they consumed the heavier food, they moved inside the gazebo with their wines and desserts. Blocking out the nuisance of insects, they could enjoy dessert and conversation under the glow of the full moon. Each couple sat in one of the love seats and Fiona gladly snuggled next to Leo.

"I hate that I'll be leaving tomorrow," Jesse said. "Work's gotta get done."

"And I love you for the sacrifice. I'll hold your position at the pool…and dinner…and your side of the bed." Belinda smiled before popping a kiss on his lips.

"I don't want to think about work, either. I should have left today." Dana stretched. "Kent and I will drive up probably on Monday."

"You needed this break, hon." Belinda's concern for her cousin showed. "You have been going at top speed."

"And your brain isn't used to that workout," Fiona joked. "It's looking for former party-girl Dana to show up."

"Be quiet, Fiona. At least I was a party girl. You were so boring." Dana snored. "You were snooze alert. Isn't that right about her, Leo?"

Leo opened his mouth to speak, but Fiona quickly craned her neck until she was close to his ear. "If you answer correctly, I'll make it worth your while." She confidently tossed a toothy grin at the others.

"She had party-girl potential," Leo began, without reacting to her whispers. "But then…"

Obviously, he needed more convincing. She continued in his ear, behind the shield of her hand, "I always wanted to trace the flight route from New York to Brazil. On your naked body. With my tongue."

His Adam's apple bobbed. "I preferred a different type of woman."

"And then I'll linger down south. Climb a tree. Admire the view. Play with the ripe fruits. And suck the juices dry." She gently kissed his ear, causing him to jump.

He sputtered. "A woman who has playful and serious sides."

Fiona reached for her glass. With exaggerated innocence, she held the straw between her fingers. Then slowly she placed her lips around the tip of the straw and sucked up the soda. After she swallowed, she licked her lips and sighed.

"Um…get a room, please." Dana threw a pillow at Fiona.

"What? I got thirsty."

Leo shook his head. "You are so…"

"Sexy?" She giggled.

"Perfect."

Chapter 7

Fiona couldn't be happier. That was how she felt with the upward trajectory of her life—her love life. The reason for her forced vacation was no longer important. She was here reconnecting with Leo in this story-book fantasy that she now desperately wanted to have a happy ending. The problem was, she couldn't tell if Leo was on the same page.

Playing at being disinterested was tough. It had been tough the first time. And the second that she saw Leo again, she'd known that it would be excruciatingly difficult. When she'd suggested to Kent that he ask Leo to be a groomsman, it had been in the secret hope that he would be in her life beyond these two weeks. She wanted him through December and beyond.

With their daily routine in place, they'd gotten sloppy with their efforts to keep their relationship hidden from the "adults." The knowing smiles and awkward run-ins as she sneaked from the guesthouse back to the main house said that she was a failure on that count. However, not one ounce of remorse poked her conscience. Maybe that was why she was still in Leo's bed during the late hours of the morning. Meanwhile, he'd dutifully gone to his regular meeting with Grace.

Eventually, Fiona clambered out of the bed, dressed in one of Leo's shirts and followed the hypnotic smell of brewed coffee. A slice of toasted bread, topped with orange marmalade, and a cup of java served as breakfast. In no hurry to go anywhere, she curled up on the couch with her food and settled in to watch TV.

An hour later, bored with the news, she wandered around the house. This man was a housekeeper's dream. His books were stacked neatly at his bedside. All his toiletries were put away in the medicine cabinet or on the shelf in the bathroom. His clothes were neatly placed in the drawers or hanging in the closet. The dining area was neat, not a stray crumb in sight. The kitchen had a bleach scent lingering in the air. After their many sessions on the counter, she could appreciate that attention to detail.

Those decadent thoughts triggered her body's arousal. She felt like a Pavlovian dog salivating at the very thought of steamy sex with Leo. She had to do something to push back the urges. It wasn't lunchtime for another hour. Leo couldn't pop over and quench her impromptu thirst.

She decided to go out on the deck and at least pretend to use her e-reader. After getting comfortable in a chair, she noticed a set of files on the chair next to hers.

Don't do it.

Fiona groaned. "Maybe just one peek."

She placed her finger on the first file and dragged it toward her. Then she took the second, third and all of them until they were fanned out on the table. No labels hinted at the contents. She'd have to flip open the files to discover the information.

Yet she hesitated. Fiona studied the arranged lot, wanting to dive in and see what on earth Leo was working on so diligently. He'd been adamant that he wouldn't share anything with her. Their conversations, no matter how she tried to control the topics, never revealed any secrets or left clues.

Sometimes, when he thought she wasn't paying attention, she'd catch him studying her. His expression would turn soft and reflective. He'd give heavy sighs, as if something weighed on his spirit. What did he want to know that he didn't or couldn't ask? A few times, she jumped on the moment and attempted to steer the conversation. Those waters were too deep. His resistance to her wading into his feelings was subtle but stood strong against her efforts.

It would be easy to believe that their connection was a wistful speck in her imagination. But in this case, she'd rely on her gut instinct, like she did for work. There was something building and growing between them. Unfortunately, she couldn't nurture what she couldn't hold on to. It would take time to gain Leo's trust. She wasn't sure that there were enough days left at the Hamptons for it to happen.

Her hand rested over the blue folder. Not many papers were stuck in each file. Still, they contained information that she was sure would assuage her curiosity.

All she had to do was flick the folder open with her thumb.

If she did, she couldn't look Leo in the eye. Climbing her way out of the hole to gain his trust was a long, tedious effort. Would she destroy all chances to regain it and his respect? The answer was a no-brainer.

But opening this file would solve a major problem. So damn tempting.

She groaned over her decision.

Finally, she replaced all the files on the seat and pushed in the chair to block them from her view. To be doubly sure that she didn't get tempted again, Fiona dressed quickly and left the guesthouse.

She hadn't snooped. Leo *could* trust her, although he'd never know how close she'd come to the discovery.

Leo had a hard time believing that he'd been given access to Grace's office. Today he was on his own. On his way there, Mrs. Finch had informed him that Grace had been called away on other business and left her office at his disposal. He couldn't admit to Mrs. Finch that he doubted the message, wondering if she'd misheard the true instructions. Grace was particular about her space. Other than short intervals when she left, she was always in the office as he worked.

He took her permission as a show of confidence, a sign that he'd earned her trust. While she had given him access to the room, she also wanted work to be done. Finding the information that she sought about her grandchild was taking longer than expected. Some parts involved a computer search. Others required he use email to retrieve information. Nothing could be hurried, even if Grace had her own timetable.

Equally important, he was on loan in the Hamptons to amend Grace's will. His career couldn't be put on hold indefinitely. And he knew that in a few days, Fiona would be returning to her home and her job. Staying on here without her held zero appeal for him.

Leo got busy with tasks at his desk. He'd taken over the small conference table in the corner of the office. In his seat, he had a row of windows behind him and along the other wall. The vantage point provided a good view of the backyard and his secret view of Fiona when she took a swim or sat in the lounge chair reading a book. Watching her wasn't distracting but rather comforting; he liked knowing that she was there. Today she wasn't outside. He wondered what time she'd sneaked back to the estate. He felt like a kid on a stealth mission, trying to beat curfew. Another reason that whatever was brewing between him and Fiona needed a different, more private playground.

His phone rang. He spent the hour finishing up with the necessary calls to establish two more trusts under Grace's foundation. Now he waited for the critical email that would turn up the pace to finding Grace's grandson.

"Where's Grace?" Verona had entered the office without knocking.

Leo jumped. "She's on another appointment."

"She left you to rifle through her stuff?"

Leo's hands paused over his keyboard. From her stance, he guessed that she was ready for a fight. He shifted and settled back in the chair. Even though he'd have loved to take the bait, he had to keep his temper in check. He had to remind himself what really was at the root of Verona's anger was Grace's action to find her grandson and reunite him with her and the rest of the family. Feeling like he were at the face-off of a grudge match, Leo took this as a challenge of his patience.

"Verona, please have a seat." Leo motioned to one of the chairs at the conference table.

"I'm not holding any discussion with you."

"Why not? I'm right here for you to ask any questions you may have. Any doubts? Bring it." He gestured for her to continue. "It's you and me in this big room. What's on your mind?"

"I know why you're doing this—it's all about the money. Connections. My daughter. You are like all the rest who come around this family and burrow in like a tick."

"Lady, you are a piece of work. Because you are the mother of the woman I love, I'll respond to you with the respect that you can't seem to show me. I will address each of your concerns. Please do not interrupt."

"You don't tell—"

Leo ignored her and pressed on. "You don't know why I'm doing this. You couldn't possibly know, because you haven't bothered to get to know me and know what my intentions are."

Her mouth turned down, and her scowl grew darker.

"I have career goals. Most people consider that normal. I have done nothing illegal to get where I am. And I haven't ever done anything unethical to stay where I am or to move ahead. Grayson, Buckley and Tynesdale law firm is my employer. Grace is a client. I'm assigned to work for her. As an employee of my firm, I have the duty to represent it to the best of my ability. And I'm damn good at what I do, or I wouldn't be here. And I certainly wouldn't be in this office unchaperoned, as you would probably phrase it."

Leo took a deep breath because he needed it. He had to set the right tone with Verona, but once he'd done so, they would be at a fork in the road. She'd either have him fired or step out of his way so he could do his job.

He continued, "As for connections?" He looked down at his hands pressed against the surface of the desk. "Yes, they matter in my business. They matter a lot. But I also am not the person to sell my soul to the highest bidder." He leaned forward, almost out of the chair, earnest with his defense. "I don't accept your insults, because they are unfair. I have done nothing to you or your family to warrant your hostility."

Silence dropped and stayed like an uninvited guest. Shock registered on her face, while Leo felt nauseous awaiting whatever next action would be taken against him.

"Maybe I was wrong in saying that. Sorry." Verona picked at her fingers.

He began softly but with a dose of determination, "As for your daughter, I have not taken advantage of Fiona."

She squinted and said, "You said that you loved her."

Leo hadn't realized that he had said the words. He hadn't dared share them with Fiona. But to bare his heart to her mother, who disliked him, was a massive risk.

"Mothers usually say, 'Don't hurt my girl.' I don't think I have that right, do you? When I will surely hurt her once the news is out." Verona wiped away the tears from her eyes.

Leo reached for a box of tissues and slid it toward

Fiona's mother. "I'll have the information that Grace wants any day now." He offered the truth.

Her sadness unraveled his irritation over her attitude. Desperation in her eyes reached out and grabbed hold of him. While he understood the pain, he also knew what could cure the fear. "It's time, Verona. Time to tell Fiona what you're so afraid will come out. I think that even before you told Grace, you worried about one day getting a phone call or a visit from your son." Leo reached across the table and gently laid his hand over hers before drawing back.

Loss had a way of slicing through the soul. He often hoped that he would get a call that it had been a big, horrific mistake and his family was still there in Brazil. That was the difference between him and his adoptive father, Franz, though.

Franz held out for hope that brought him comfort. While, he held on to dread that was a different beast— one that sucked the essence out of every connection to and from a person.

"Thank you, Leo." Now she openly cried into her hands. "Thank you."

He hurried around the conference table and sat next to her, guiding her head to his shoulder. "We've both got your daughter's best interest at heart. She knows you're hurting."

She nodded. Her sobs had turned into loud sniffles.

Leo looked at his watch. It was noon, around the time for him to head back to the guesthouse for his special lunch break with Fiona. "I know you don't want her to see you like this. Let me leave the room first. I'll find her and keep her busy so you can leave without the attention."

He shut down his computer. He didn't bother to check for incoming emails. Today he'd pause in his duties. They all needed to take a breather.

He exited the office without looking back. A weight had lifted. While he hadn't started out feeling appreciation for Verona, his mind-set had shifted. He'd judged her actions and decision as a young adult through the prism of his own pain and anger. This brutally honest chat helped them both. She'd kicked in his defenses like an angry mama bear and demanded some truths from him, especially about her daughter.

Now to find Fiona and take her off the premises so Verona could pull herself together.

Their customary lunch romp, as he and Fiona called it, started with him heading to the guesthouse the same way he entered the estate, through the house by way of the garage. Fiona would already be at the guesthouse or would arrive soon after him.

Being slightly early, he wasn't sure if she was still in the house. As he emerged in the hallway, he checked his watch again and then peered down the hallway for signs of anyone. Voices rose and lowered as the residents and staff went about their business. He looked over his shoulder at the office door to make sure that Verona hadn't grown impatient and come out. The door remained closed. Taking a deep breath, Leo picked up his pace and headed down the hallway toward the kitchen.

"Leo?" Fiona leaned over the second-floor rail. "Wait up." It didn't take long for her to meet him at the bottom of the stairs and plant a kiss on his mouth. "Figured I could intercept and have us haul ass upstairs." She giggled and started pulling him toward the stairs.

He shook his head. "Come with me." Leo tried to keep his tone calm.

"No. Let's sneak upstairs." She ran halfway up the steps ahead of him.

"Not today."

"Oh?" She walked back down toward him. "What's wrong?"

Why did she have to look so fresh and inviting? The pink hibiscus flower in her hair was a nice touch.

"Nothing. It's been a long day. I feel like heading out. Get some air, clear my head."

"Something's bothering you. I can tell. I can read it in your face. Is everything okay?" She kept speaking, growing more insistent. "I know Grace went out with Henry. Mrs. Finch said that he wasn't feeling good."

That was news. Verona probably hadn't known that her father was ill when she came to the office. Leo worked to remove any sense of alarm. "I hope your grandfather isn't sick. But everything is fine with me."

"I don't believe you. But I won't argue anymore. Let me go get my purse and the keys." She started up the stairs again. Over her shoulder, she said, "Maybe one day, you'll feel that you can trust me. I've turned into a good listener."

Leo didn't answer, not that Fiona had waited for a response. He took a seat on the last step and waited for her. Frankly, he was a bit surprised that she'd brought up the topic of trust. That subject was more than a minefield; it was rather like quicksand. What they had now was good and consistent. Soon it would be a complete mess.

"Ready?" Fiona jingled the car keys.

They walked out together toward Fiona's car. The

heat wave that had gripped the area had dissipated. Now the weather didn't hold the burden of humidity. Leo was thankful for the slight breeze as his gaze took in the overcast sky. The promise of rain was welcomed.

Fiona turned off the radio, turned up the AC and hit the gas.

Leo barely had time to click in his seat belt. He glanced over to read her mood. The speedometer hit thirty…forty…fifty with a screech of tires as they rounded a curve.

"I only wanted fresh air, maybe lunch. I could do without an emergency trip to the hospital."

"Sorry." Her foot eased off the gas.

His abs unclenched and he relaxed his grip on the door handle. "What was that all about?"

"Dunno." She swept back her hair and propped her head on her hand. She alternated between looking at him and the road. "A little bit of frustration getting in the way."

"About…?" He stared straight ahead, hoping she would approach the next bend with more caution.

"You're having a bad day, so you want to be with me. I'm more than a lunch booty call and a shoulder to cry on."

Tires squealed again on a curve.

"I agree. So you don't think that you're taking advantage of me?"

Whiplash. Had she just stopped in the middle of the road? Yes, this was a private drive, but still, what the heck?

Leo jumped in before she had a chance to unleash on him. "Before you go *diablo* on me and add to the crick in my neck, let me clarify that you implied that I was enjoying you and your body as a one-way benefit. Wouldn't you agree that when you are having a bad day, you come to me because I am the best hugger? I give great shoulder and back rubs. And my advice is worthy of your appreciation."

She nodded. Yet her mouth was tight. Her hands wringing the steering wheel.

"Do you not say in the throes of pleasure, 'Leo, do it. Do it, Leo. Yes, that's it. Right there. You the man'?" His falsetto drew a small smile from her.

"I don't sound like that." She laughed outright. "And I did not say 'You the man.'"

He leaned over and playfully tugged her earlobe. "But I am your man, right?"

She nodded and then resumed driving.

"It was a busy morning, that's all," Leo added.

"Would you rather have been alone? Don't worry—it's not a trick question. I know sometimes being in a quiet place without people and things distracting you is helpful."

"Not at all. I did want us to head out to lunch."

"Where do you want to go?"

"I don't know." And he truly didn't know. He glanced over to her, knowing that he was responsible for the concern that slid into place on her face. The earlier exuberance had disappeared. "Just want to be with you." He held her hand and brought it to his lips. "You're beautiful."

"Thank you, my sexy lover." She kissed his finger, bathing it with her tongue. "Sure you don't want to head back to the house?"

"You are making it darn difficult to concentrate."

"Then I'm going to rehabilitate you."

"Oh, really?" He had to hang on to the dashboard as she gunned the engine and headed to parts unknown. Leo kept an eye on the street signs, but they meant nothing to him. "Am I being kidnapped?"

"You could say that." She smiled and he knew that everything would be all right.

They headed through town and beyond its outskirts, where a general store and a few antiques shops lined the sides of the road. After they passed a gas station and the one traffic light for the town, Fiona pulled into a hotel parking lot.

Leo scanned the area. "I hate to ask, but is this going to be a sex stop?"

"Wouldn't you like to know?"

The place looked fairly decent. A few cars were parked in its lot. Given its proximity to Southampton, the property was probably a cheaper option since it was outside town.

"We don't have reservations." Leo stated the obvious.

"Ah… we don't need one. I did reconnaissance and thought that this would be ideal for a getaway treat. Didn't know that I'd need to make use of it so quickly." She pulled up in the half-empty lot and cut the engine. "Are you getting out? I don't plan to have fun all by my lonesome."

Leo still looked around, hoping to see one person walking down the hallway or going to the diner across the street. "Where are the people?"

"Hurry up." She was out the door and headed to the front entrance. Her hair bounced with each step, with a little help from the sway of her hips. The woman could rock a pair of shorts.

Leo chuckled. His woman was so damned cool with a lot of badassness.

She got a room key, which dangled from her finger. The front-desk clerk had to know what they were up to with no luggage and Fiona's come-hither glances at Leo.

Not that Leo cared what the guy thought. When Fiona beckoned him into the elevator cab, he didn't hesitate. It was tiny for two people. Three would have been a tad intimate. He noted their final destination—third floor.

She held her place in the elevator as he brushed past her to his spot. The doors had barely closed when her hands slid behind her back. Leo felt the anticipation of something. He looked up at the light switching from one floor to the next.

He sucked in a deep breath.

Her hand slowly cupped him between the legs.

A soft squeeze to his balls. Her palm circled his arousal, then her fingers massaged him into exquisite delirium.

He groaned, the agony making it sound more like a growl. His heart pulsed at frenetic speed. The elevator was taking too long to get to the third floor. Any longer and he'd be ready to push the emergency stop button, kiss the back of Fiona's neck and take her right there. His right leg spasmed, as if ready to make it happen.

Finally, the doors pinged, almost sending his nerves out of his skin. They barely made it in the room, pulling off each other's clothes, kissing and grinding their bodies in a silent erotic message.

Leo loved this woman who moved in sync with his desire. In exchange, he served her desires and her needs. She lay on her side with her hair spread like a fan on the pillow. Perfection. He climbed into bed behind her, smoothly coming to rest against her silky skin. With his hand holding her hip, with condom on, he entered her wet sex, savoring the warm walls like a sheath around his arousal. He slid his hand between her legs, stimulating her clit to please her. Their bodies moved together in a sensual partnership. Leo continued to rub her clit, enjoying her wetness for him. He wanted her satisfied. He wanted her to climax. He didn't stop teasing her as he kissed her shoulder. She bucked her hips against his pelvis. His fingers stroked and played intimately with her. He anticipated her release and brought her to the edge, then pulled her back, only to rush her to the edge with greater intensity. The room filled with her ragged breaths and soft moans in answer to his touch. When she couldn't take it any longer, her hand grabbed his wrist in a tight vise. Soon after, her orgasm took hold of her and sent out waves of contractions against his arousal.

"Your turn, baby."

"As you wish…" Leo let go—hard. Eyes squeezed shut. Toes curled tight. He soared, gripping her hips for dear life. The liftoff was steep and belly dropping. His release rendered him speechless but still able to manage a few deep-throated grunts.

"Lunch was delish, baby," Fiona whispered.

"Yeah? Well, I want seconds."

She giggled as he peppered her neck with kisses.

Back at the house and in her room, Fiona still glowed from her lunchtime romp with Leo. It was all she could think about as they watched TV. She was surprised that he hadn't rushed back to Grace's office but wasn't going to mention anything.

"Let's make a deal," she said.

"Okay."

"Let's not call this time at the Hamptons the end." Fiona muted the TV.

"What do you want to call it?"

"Part one." She studied him for a reaction. His calmness unnerved her.

"And how many parts are there?"

"Two parts. And the second part can go on for a… very…long time."

He made a face as if pondering the idea. "Sounds reasonable."

"That's it?" She pushed his thigh, not sure how to feel about his easygoing response over something that was important.

He turned toward her. The look of amusement disappeared. "Only need to know how far you're willing to take it this time. Short haul. Long haul."

She was peeved that he kept referencing the past.

"I thought you'd ask me to be your girlfriend for the long term."

"Are you really ready?"

Fiona didn't jump to answer immediately. "I didn't start out knowing exactly what I wanted or how you'd react to me. I know we're still working on getting to know each other.

"*Trusting* each other."

"Yes, trust is important. But I'm ready for all of it." Fiona felt like she was negotiating for her life.

"I'll take you at your word, then."

She kissed him and said against his lips, "Then let's seal the deal."

Chapter 8

Instead of the usual jog the next morning, Leo opted for a brisk walk along the Shinnecock Bay with its white sandy beach and blue waters. Boaters were up early and making their way to their destinations. He wasn't the type to expound about the spiritual effects of water and its power over his mood. Such a philosophy was too close to the deeply held beliefs of his people and their interconnectedness to nature. And look where it got them when a massive flood and mudslide wiped them out in less than a day. He picked up driftwood and tossed it into the water, then watched it move with the current. Maybe the wood would float out into the Atlantic Ocean.

Leo noticed he suddenly had company. "Hey, fella, what are you doing out here by yourself?"

A small dog wagged its tail. Its mouth curved in a wet smile with its tongue lolling to the side.

"Lost?" He looked around for signs of anyone, but the beach was deserted. "I'm sure you shouldn't be here." Leo couldn't boast about knowing what the steps were after finding a dog. Although, in this case, he felt that the dog had found him. "Are you a beagle? Kind of look like one." He should have watched more Westminster Kennel shows. Were beagles friendly?

The dog kept an attentive gaze on him, but it didn't move from the spot it had occupied since arriving on the scene.

"I need to look at your collar." He held out his hands, unsure if palms up or palms down meant anything. But he kept a wary eye for any shift from the dog's subdued curiosity to the bared fangs of a hellhound.

Leo moved slowly, hoping to gain the dog's trust. They didn't have the luxury of long hours to bond. He offered his hand for the dog to sniff. Its wet nose brushed across his knuckles, followed by a quick lick. *Success.* They had passed the greeting stage. Leo grinned. His new friend did a happy dance of wagging its tail at a feverish pace and running in wide circles around him. Leo reached down and managed a few head scratches when the dog paused for the attention. Its excited yips filled the air. Eventually, Leo held the dog and checked the small tag that hung from the collar. He read off the phone number and pulled out his cell to dial.

No one answered. But he heard a phone ringing nearby and a voice calling.

The dog's ears immediately perked up and its head turned toward the caller. Without so much as a goodbye wag of its tail, the little animal took off and disappeared over a grassy dune.

A car approached on his trek toward the road. Headlights blinked on and off. As it drew close, he recognized the car and driver. He waved for Fiona to pull over and slid into the car.

"Thought I might see you on your run. I was headed on a quick errand."

"I was playing with a lost pup. But he or she found its owner. Then I was abandoned."

"Who wouldn't want to play with you?" she asked in exaggerated baby talk.

"Not any four-legged friends."

"You got me." She mussed his hair.

"Yeah, I do." Leo settled into the seat with a small smile. He and his woman with their dog or cat to make the unit complete. He almost nodded over the pleasing image.

"Coming with me on my errand?"

He shook his head. "Unfortunately, I need for you to hit the gas? I'll be late for work, but maybe I can cut it down by thirty minutes."

"You don't jump to attention with me. I'm jealous."

"You aren't paying me," he teased.

"Oh, it's like that now. I'll walk with my wallet for the next time."

"Guess I'll be the one paying for that remark."

She nodded. Her grin was wicked and fun.

They came to a stop in front of the house. Time for him to get his head back on his job.

"We'll talk later." He leaned over and gently popped a kiss on her waiting mouth.

"Before you go, I've got something on my mind." She bit her lip, before continuing, "I never apologized for putting an end to us. I'm sorry."

"Thank you."

"We're a work in progress, right?" Her smile trembled.

"I'm looking forward to getting it right with you, baby." He kissed her hard, her mouth sweet and hungry for his tongue. He stroked her, relishing her equal passion. All was not lost. As he pulled back to leave, he truly wanted to believe the look in her eyes that seemed to match what he felt. That they would be all right.

Another day slipped by and if she could sing, Fiona would have belted out a song to rival any musical number. Whistling an upbeat tune, she popped her head into the dining room to see if anyone was in there. Everything was quiet. No sign of anyone. She'd hoped that as the days dwindled down and her departure on Saturday neared, she could spend a lot of time with Leo. But the closed-door sessions with Grace were longer and his attitude even more intense. She couldn't get time with him to throw out her invitation for another hotel getaway.

So instead she had roped in Belinda to help her do the gardening for Grandpa Henry. Even Cassie, her great-aunt, joined in. Right now, she wasn't sure how much weeding and mulching got done, as she surveyed the area. But there was a lot of laughter and merriment among the group that she appreciated. And now with her grandfather having to take it easy, he couldn't dodge her questions like he'd done all through the last week.

"Looks like fun." Verona stood just outside their circle. "May I join you?" She wasn't really dressed for digging in the dirt, but Fiona seized the suggestion.

"We are cleaning up some areas." Fiona stepped aside for her mother to join them and close the circle. "And Dad?"

"He has one of his migraines. He's lying down."

Much of her childhood was spent witnessing her father suffer from crippling headaches. Staying quiet had been her special job. She'd wanted to be the best at it and earn the treats he'd give her when he was better.

"I'll go see him later if he's better."

"He'd like that." Verona offered a smile laced with sadness.

Her mother wasn't a weeping willow. Growing up with Verona's emotional distance hadn't bothered Fiona at first. Hadn't been until she visited her school friends at their homes that she saw the Starks contrasts with her family. They lived a life of polite indifference. Expressing feelings was not discouraged but was not a frequent occurrence. The hugs and kisses to the head she'd received for a job well done or to raise her spirits after a bad experience could be counted on one hand. By the time she was in college, she barely went home for the holidays. It would take Grace's mandated family events to get her back home. Despite it all, she considered her life normal. Trading it in for someone else's wasn't realistic. Besides, her family's attitude had its perks. It kept her in a position of never having to share her feelings, shielding her from the possibility of disappointment.

"When you were a little girl, we planted a tree together. You, me and your father—a cherry tree."

"Really? I don't remember..." Fiona recalled the events in which her entire family had participated—not many.

"You were probably three years old." Her mother wiped her brow. "Unfortunately, the tree died. I think it was beetles.

"Why a cherry tree?"

"It's about life." Verona remained in her squatting position, pulling out the weeds. "Life is beautiful and fragile."

"You sound like a poet."

Her mother laughed. "Far from it. It was my stint in Japan."

"Japan? When did you go to Japan?"

"When I was in college."

"Grandpa, you never told me that Mom was in Japan."

He grunted. "I think that I'd better get in the shade." He walked away, leaving Fiona to frown at his abrupt departure.

"You should tell me about Japan, Mom."

"Yes." Verona was suddenly intent on weed removal.

Fiona wasn't holding her breath that she'd learn about her mom's adventures in Japan. But she had to admit that her mother didn't have to share the information. Observing such tenderness in her mother's face, the gentle encouragement in her tone, the hand that lingered on her arm—every act made her yearn for more. Dare she hope that the Hamptons estate had enough magic to not only give her Leo but reconnect her with her mother?

This garden plot had been Cassie's dream of an area designed by the family. Fiona remembered her mother and aunts creating the garden once the professional landscaper had done the heavy, backbreaking work. Tending the garden was another chance for family bonding. The three generations—well, minus

Grandpa Henry—spent another hour digging through the dirt, pulling out the dead plants and shifting the landscaping rocks to form a more decorative boundary.

"Well, this has killed my back," Belinda complained. She stretched her spine, wincing as she moved from side to side. "But I'm putting this on Instagram." She pulled off her gloves and then positioned her camera to take several photos that had every family member scrambling out of the shot.

"A massage would be lovely," Cassie said. "I love my gardens, too, but after the guys come and work on it."

"I know what you mean," Verona remarked as she watched Henry return with a drink to sit under the patio umbrella.

"Dad, you shouldn't be out here. I know you went to the doctor yesterday."

"And I'm fine." He sipped his drink.

"What did the doctor say, Grandpa?" Fiona asked.

"That he should stop eating all those sugary foods and carbs." Cassie shook her head at him. "I told Mrs. Finch to change the meals for him."

"Means tasteless food." Henry scowled.

"We want you here with us for a long time." Fiona didn't want to think about her dear grandfather being ill.

"Okay, everyone stop fussing. Let's move inside, where it's cooler." Henry pushed up slowly from the chair and shuffled into the house.

"Um… Fiona, could we talk, please?" Her mother looked like she had walked into a sauna.

"Are you feeling all right?" Fiona left her grandfather's side and rushed to her mother.

"I'm fine." She didn't look fine. "Let's go to the sitting room."

Fiona would rather have had a chance to clean up, but her mother's request had a flavor of urgency and desperation. Instead she walked beside her to the sitting room opposite Grace's office. She looked toward the door, hoping that Leo would open it. The expression on her mother's face was tense, a mood that wasn't unusual. Verona could be considered high maintenance. But along with the tension, there was a heaviness that seemed to suck the life out of her.

"Have a seat, Fiona. Guess it's kind of obvious that I have something important to tell you." Verona wrung her hands. Her mouth widened for a smile, but it didn't resemble one.

"Are you sick? Is Dad sick?"

Her mother shook her head. "This isn't about any illness. It's about the family."

Fiona bit her lip. More questions came to mind. Trying to stay calm, she sucked in the impulse to go through an interrogation process. From her mother's unsettled demeanor, Fiona knew in her heart that she would not like the news. Only thing to do now was hold tight to the growing dread and pray that her mother would not drag out whatever she had to say.

"Many years ago, while I was in college, I was pregnant." Verona waited for her reaction.

"And…?" Fiona said one word, while her thoughts rambled like an avalanche with questions, feelings, surprise and apprehension.

"You have a brother. Dresden." Her mother, who always looked retro in her style and self-possessed attitude, could have blended into a 1950s TV drama with ease. But not while delivering this latest news.

"And…?"

"I gave him up for adoption."

"How could Grace do that?" Fiona didn't attempt to dial back her instant anger at her grandmother's interference. Now it made sense why Grace and her mother looked ready for battle.

"She didn't make me do anything." Verona rubbed at her forehead. She hadn't looked Fiona in the eyes since she'd started speaking. "Grace didn't know. Not even my sisters. Only Aunt Cassie."

"Cassie?" Apparently, Fiona could only manage one-word responses, while her mind reeled from the myriad of thoughts forming and reforming in an effort to help her understand.

Verona nodded. "After college I married your dad and we lived our lives."

"Does he know?"

"Yes. I told him when we dated. The guilt gnawed at me and I couldn't feel normal, because it was such a secret. I didn't know how to tell my mother, who expected so much from me, that I had done this. I put my child up for adoption because I felt like a failure to get pregnant. Heck, for having sex. And I didn't want the news to get out and be made a symbol as my mother was making headlines as a role model for women. I handled it on my own."

"More like with Cassie's help." Fiona didn't know whether to be angry with her aunt for helping or at her mother. But she didn't know how to be angry at either woman without feeling that she was letting down those who'd had to follow through on actions that would make her weak in the knees.

Fiona stood and walked around the room. She needed to keep moving. Her feet kept going until she opened the door and stepped into the hallway. Only then did she inhale a sobering breath.

This morning, the only major issue on her mind had been a former boyfriend. How were she and Leo going to reconcile? Emotionally, she'd thought that was enough of a burden to solve.

Now within the last few minutes, she'd been hit with a revelation that touched so many lives. Touched her life. She had a brother, a person she didn't know. And her mother, who she'd thought was ideally perfect, albeit emotionally cool, had blown up that goddess status. She was normal, like her.

Fiona went back into the room. She resumed her seat.

"Grace hired Leo to find your brother. She wants contact. She wants to bring him into the family fold. There will be a will change. But don't worry—you'll be fine."

"I don't give a hoot about the will!" Fiona screamed. She was back on her feet and racing out of the room. A will would never be the instrument used to threaten or reward her.

But more importantly, Leo *knew* this secret.

And he'd kept it from her, while he had the task to amend the will and probably to facilitate the family reunification. Well, they could plan all they wanted. She wasn't participating in this circus. She stormed back into the room.

"I can't turn back what I've done." Verona now

raised her gaze to Fiona, who didn't return to her seat. "But I ask that you don't judge harshly. Life has a way of giving us tests, and when we fail, we have three choices. We can correct ourselves, we can continue the same mistake, or we can do nothing and pretend or hope that it goes away. I want to do nothing. I'd like to bury my head in the sand dune out there until all of this has blown over. But my own cowardice for giving up the baby did this. I picked the easy solution for me. So I will work with Grace to correct whatever I can."

"Good for you, Mom. But, I'm going to need a minute to digest everything." Fiona felt as if she couldn't possibly take in any more news.

"Okay," Verona replied.

Fiona worked with families searching for their loved ones. More times than not, they were ecstatic when they learned the whereabouts of their loved ones, even in cases where the outcome was a sad one. The closure was what was needed. Then why wasn't she ecstatic about the news of her missing brother, who also had been found?

Leo couldn't stop staring at the photo of the man who was Grace's only grandson. Dresden Haynes. He had to admit that he'd thought Dresden would have the tall, slender physique of the Meadows women. Even Henry, and who now battled with his body's traitorous spread, had been a tall, gawky young man in his younger days. Not so with Dresden.

Muscles were all over this guy. He had either bodybuilding or professional wrestling on his horizon. The man standing in an all-black suit with dark shades to match looked like the too-cool-for-school type. Yet Leo couldn't make any conclusions about the guy. Except that it was more than a cosmic coincidence that he, as a bodyguard, had taken on a profession as a protector, like Fiona.

The biographical details provided by his firm's recommended PI had been committed to memory before he turned over the information to Grace. Reading the information had filled him with nervous anticipation. His concern wasn't about Grace or even Verona's reaction. Fiona filled his thoughts. While he knew that one day soon she would be told, he nevertheless dreaded the very minute when she learned the truth. He hoped that the tumultuous mix of anger and joy, confusion and acceptance, would give way to healing. Both mother and daughter would need support from each other.

"I like the name—Dresden," Grace said. She hadn't put down the file since he handed it to her. She read aloud. "It says here Dresden Haynes had no other siblings and was adopted by an older couple who had been living on a US military base in Japan. The parents now lived in Florida, while his current address is unknown."

While Dresden's background was interesting, the focal point of Leo's interest was the photo. There was no doubt that Dresden and Fiona were siblings. It didn't matter that they didn't share the same father. Similar features from their mother and their grandmother came through in brother and sister.

Leo suspected that Grace had already read it several times, committing all the details to heart.

"I want to meet him as soon as possible. I will send the jet wherever and whenever to make it happen."

"I think you should take things slow," he cautioned.

She nodded, but the joy in her eyes reflected the temptation to go against his wishes.

"I don't want you to get your hopes up before I've had a chance to make contact." Leo didn't want to remind her that this wasn't a business acquisition, where she might be perceived as the hero. This was a real person who could condemn her actions.

"I understand. I'm so eager that I'm not thinking that he wouldn't want to see me."

"We don't know if his parents told him about the adoption. And…we don't know if they would protest such a move if they didn't."

"He's an adult. He's four years older than Fiona."

What Leo didn't say but also considered as a scenario: *If he knew, in all that time, he never made an attempt to contact you or Verona.*

Grace waved off his report. "That's why I have you working on this, Leo—to make it happen. You understand. You know how to be sensitive. I don't care about the past. I can't do a damn thing about it. But from this day forward, I can do everything in my power to have my family whole again. And that is my birthday wish to myself. I want to meet him."

"Grace, I think that this part of the project should come from someone close to the family."

"Wouldn't that be you, Leo?" Her eyebrow cocked as if the answer was a given. "You are close to everyone. And you are close to Fiona. That's why I'm volunteering you. I need someone who can be strong but sensitive to the client's needs."

"Don't use Fiona to manipulate me."

"Because you fancy her? And you're afraid of what she'll think?"

Leo remembered Fiona's advice that Grace was testing him. But the term *fancy* sounded so temporary. "It's not a fancy." This seemed like a day for revelations.

"I would hope not. My granddaughters are perfectly capable of picking their partners. I may have my opinions, but I don't intervene with relationships. Lord knows I've done my own thing."

Leo exhaled a sigh of relief. "Thank you. I feel better about not having to sneak around."

"Not that either of you were great at sneaking. Let me put it this way—I would not recruit you and Fiona for any clandestine operation." She chuckled.

"But I haven't done a bad job with this case." His face was warm from embarrassment.

"You're absolutely right. But that's why you should contact Dresden."

"And I insist that someone in the family make the first contact."

"Why?"

"For thirty-six years, this man has had no contact with any of you. You don't know what he's been told. And I think that you should make the effort to contact his parents. While it would be easier to send someone with no connection to the family, it also would be easier for him to shut the door on all of this."

Defiance squared her shoulders. Her mouth flattened in a straight line. Determination glittered in her eyes. "I'll write the letter. You will deliver it."

Leo wasn't keen on being the deliveryman, but this was a little better than him knocking on the door with a story that could get him punched in the face.

Chapter 9

Fiona didn't wait to talk to Leo. She'd sucked in her breath and reached deep for enough courage to ask Grace for Dresden's information. It was one of the rare times that Grace merely nodded and handed over the file with a look that could be sympathy. But Fiona didn't want anything but the information.

With Dresden's information in her hand, she could run a check on him to get his current address. No one wanted her to contact him before Grace had a chance to make the official introduction with him via Leo. She hadn't planned as far ahead as meeting him. Every few minutes, the new reality set in again that she had a brother. Now that she'd thought about having a meetup, she felt lighter about the entire situation. Besides, her brother carried zero responsibility for any of her misgivings over this revelation. But she couldn't deny that she had lots of questions for Leo.

She'd managed to avoid Leo the few times that he emerged from Grace's office. Of course, he had no idea what she'd learned, or at least, she didn't think so.

Since feelings were raw, she didn't want to jump to conclusions. Belinda's high-road mantra still echoed. To guarantee that she stuck to the sentiment, Fiona went to her room to start packing. The curtain was closing on the Southampton vacation in a way that she couldn't have predicted, with feelings that she never thought would have a second chance and with an anticipation of what would be next.

Her nightmares and restless frustration over her career had diminished. Being out of that environment had helped a lot and she would blow her captain's mind when she returned with an apology and acknowledgment of his rehabilitative wisdom.

But only one smidgen of doubt about what she was doing with her life, in comparison to her cousins, was enough to generate a crisis of faith in her profession. Should she be honing an entrepreneurial spirit and conquering some unknown land with her skills? She'd landed at the door of the estate almost two weeks ago, ready to chuck it in, but with no idea of what to do. But she'd felt compelled to think of or do something. As her anxiety quieted and the other parts of her soul settled, healed and grew stronger, she'd stopped engaging the idea that she hadn't found the job for her. She was a detective for Missing Persons. She was good at her job. She caught predators. She reunited families. Ultimately, that was her goal every time she worked on a case: reuniting, reconnecting, shoring up family bonds, even if the missing had passed on.

The message of her mother's cherry tree, to treasure the beauty and fragility of life, couldn't have come at a better time. Fiona sighed and hoped that her mother could have closure now.

"Dresden," she said to the empty room. "I know my mother never stopped thinking about you, never stopped loving you."

"Hey, baby." Leo tested the ground with a soft greeting. "You're here." He was glad that she was in the guesthouse.

"Why wouldn't I be?" Fiona smiled at him from his bed and his insides melted.

"Well, I didn't know how you were doing after the news. Verona shared that she'd told you. She was worried when you disappeared." He kissed her lips, still not sure of her mood. "I tried to find you."

"Had a quick run to make with Belinda." She made a face. "I have to head back tomorrow."

"Tomorrow?" Regardless of what she said, he knew this had to do with the news of her brother. "I was hoping to spend this final weekend with you."

"Me, too, baby."

"Is it an emergency?"

"Belinda has to get back for a big meeting. She came up with Dana."

He nodded.

"It's not like this is the end. When you're done with everything here, you know where to find me."

"Yeah." Yet hearing of her sudden departure unsettled him. Here was the real test of whether they had truly turned the corner and were headed for a smooth ride for their relationship after they left this magical Hamptons setting.

"Baby, stop frowning. I'll run a bath for you."

He nodded.

She hopped out of bed in a lingerie number that tied in the front but covered her upper body in a red see-through curtain. The bottom half was a string bikini that was more string than material, allowing for full appreciation of the small curve of her behind as she walked into the bathroom.

He heard the water running and various bottles being snapped open and closed as she administered to the bath experience. It took only seconds to peel off his clothes and toss them to a nearby chair. Naked and aroused, he couldn't wait to dive into the water. His goal was to get her out of her sexy lingerie and make fierce love to her.

"Ready?" Her hand trailed along the scented soapy suds covering the water.

Leo took a tentative toe dip before sinking his body gratefully into the warm water. The magic of the temperature instantly loosened his muscles. He submerged his body underwater with a sigh. "You can join me. This tub is like an ocean liner."

"I want to bathe you."

"And I can't wait."

She pointed the remote and lowered the lights, and the faux candles around the tub glimmered with their wavering light. Soft music played through the hidden speakers. A hint of mint perfumed the air.

"Lie back and close your eyes." She laid a dry washcloth over his closed lids.

Leo complied, relaxed but still looking forward to what she was going to do; his senses were on alert.

"I'm going to start with a scrub."

He almost whimpered under her first touch. She talked her way through scrubbing him, starting with his chest and moving up and along his shoulders. Her voice continued to soothe him.

"You can't leave tomorrow."

"That's why I'm giving you this goodbye gift." She slid the washcloth down his body and over his arousal. "I want your body to remember me. Every inch of you must have a reminder of me."

He hissed. The circular motion around his shaft and over his balls sent an electric jolt. He sat up and the washcloth fell off into the water.

"You've got to keep your eyes closed."

It wasn't that he didn't trust her. But damn if his nerves weren't on edge with anticipation. Every inch of skin reacted to her touch as if hit by a Taser gun at regular intervals.

Like now. The washcloth washed the length of his legs, and without warning, her other hand grabbed his shaft and offered a slight squeeze.

Leo's eyelids snapped open. His hand slid into the water with a splash.

"Just checking to see if you're awake."

"Yes." His response dragged out into a ragged hiss.

"Let's wash you off and then a nice massage is coming right up to get the blood pumping."

"Um… I don't think that I need any help with any part of me pumping."

She smiled with a seductive curve to her lips that stirred his imagination for what would come later.

Using the extended cord of the showerhead, she hosed him down. His legs shook as she took her time washing his crotch.

He reached for the towel as soon as the water was off. He needed a moment to breathe again.

"No, I've got it." She took the towel and vigorously rubbed his skin dry.

Then her mouth slid over his shaft, to the hilt.

"Holy…" His hand shot out to the wall for support. His knees almost buckled.

She worked him. Her tongue owned him.

Every stroke along the sensitive skin seized him, building the tension, making him almost go on tiptoe. Her tongue caressed and brushed his head. And just as suddenly, she released him.

It took a few seconds for his brain to function, for speech to reach his vocal cords, for his heart rate to readjust so that he didn't pass out.

Leo tried to take a step back, but not before her mouth reclaimed his shaft. Her attention had been missed in its brief absence. When the warmth of her mouth enveloped his length, he wanted to weep with relief. But she wouldn't let him be. She wouldn't let him fall into the sweet abyss of sexual foreplay.

As long as she sucked him, draining him, teasing him, his responses were strained groans pushing free from his throat. His hand lightly cupped her head, letting her set the pace. His balls tightened. His butt clenched.

Abruptly, her mouth went slack, reversing its movement over his shaft, retreating with slow deliberation. He looked down, hoping that maybe she was ready to slip her sex over his member.

"You're killing me," he complained.

"Not yet...not yet." She kissed the tip and licked the glistening moisture. "My skills might need honing."

"I don't mind helping you get them right. I'll stay after school for extra lessons."

"You're going to be my willing subject?"

"Willing and ready." Leo was ready to pop.

Self-control wasn't something that he could brag about when her lingerie was now soaked against her skin. Her bare skin was delicious, but with the wet, gauzy material outlining the contours of her breasts and peaked nipples, she looked good. Every time he reached for her, she stepped out of the way. Her smile let him know that she was quite aware of what she was doing. He'd play her game until they got to the bed. Then no more games.

"What are you thinking?" she asked.

"You don't want to know." His nostrils flared. The addictive scent of her perfume mixed with the clean smell of her skin. He wanted to lick her entire body.

"Time for more pampering on the bed."

"Can I take a pass?" he whined. Once more he reached for her as she walked ahead of him to the bedroom.

She pushed his hands away from her hips. Her laughter at his attempts did nothing to quell his passion or desire to try again.

"I repeat, you're killing me."

"I know CPR."

He reached for her again, encircling her with his arms. They fell onto the bed, with him on top of her. Her behind wiggled against him. She made no effort to subdue her giggles over his misery. He kissed the graceful line of her back. Once the intimate contact was made, there was no turning back.

"What about your massage?"

"There are other ways you can massage me." He slid off the bed and hiked up her lingerie. "Or I can massage you." His finger slipped under the string, following its path along the split of her cheeks and the moist opening of her sex. He lingered, rubbing his knuckle against the sensitive flesh, listening to her breath hitch, watching her backside perk up. It was his turn to deliver revenge.

"Wait…" she gasped. "I'm not done with you."

"That may be, sweetheart, but you're going to put a rain check on your delivery." He spread her cheeks and delivered a precise trace of the string bikini with his tongue. Her juice flowed, sweet, from her sex. His hand gripped her behind, kneading the firm curve as he played with her clit. "Take it off."

She remained on her knees, leaning over the bed as she pushed down the pile of string from her lower body. He helped her remove it from around her ankles. Now she was free for his devouring. His appetite roared over the upcoming meal.

Nothing else tasted so sweet. His tongue lapped at her essence as it poured for him.

Leo loved this woman with everything he had in him. This time he'd do things right, so she'd never want to leave.

Fiona walked out of the room three times. On the third departure, she didn't return to listen to more of her mother's confession. It took two days for her mother to tell the story. She needed space and time to digest the news. Emotions slammed in and out of her, alternating in a manic mix of turmoil and panic. Did she have a right to feel anything but happy and overjoyed at the shocking revelation of a brother?

She paced outside the room, up and down the hallway, muttering to herself. Mrs. Finch was directing the housekeeping staff to tackle the entryway and staircase. Though the house manager acknowledged her with only the briefest of nods, Fiona knew Mrs. Finch had the keen knack to read her, and probably the entire family. But she'd never interject herself into their personal business.

The muted sound of a ringing phone from across the hallway drew Fiona's attention to her grandmother's office. She faced the closed door with balled fists.

Her mother or Grace? Leo? She needed to yell at someone. Or she could walk it off, an option that was probably better for her survival than pitching a fit at any one of them.

Fiona ran up to her room. She snatched her keys, wiped away the tears and grabbed her pocketbook. For a second, she thought about her mother waiting in the sitting room. But she couldn't go back in there. A break from listening to her mother's secret and the reason for her decision would allow time for Fiona's reaction and an all-out emotional rant. No way could she deal with her mother now.

She headed for the stairs and then wanted to get out of the house.

"Hey, what's the matter?" Belinda asked, grabbing Fiona's arm as she tried to rush past her.

"I've got to get out of here."

"All right. But I'm going with you. And I will drive." Belinda plucked the keys out of Fiona's hands.

"I'm fine. And I don't need a babysitter."

"From the look on your face, you look like you need a drink."

"Make that plural," Fiona muttered.

"And that's why I need to drive."

Fiona appreciated the comforting arm that Belinda placed around her shoulder. Right now she was on autopilot; her feet moved of their own accord out the front door and to the car.

"Did you want to let Leo know what's up?"

Fiona shook her head.

"All right. Don't shake your head off your neck."

As they drove away, Fiona had to admit that her cousin's company might be the right medicine. She slumped down in the seat and listened to music while the scenery slipped by unnoticed.

"Ready to talk?" Belinda drove a familiar route.

"When we get to the beach." Fiona closed her eyes, wishing that she could also pull down the shutter on her thoughts. Really, she wasn't sure what she was supposed to feel. And she didn't want anyone telling her how to respond to the news.

"Getting out?" Belinda prompted when they arrived at the beach.

"Sure." Fiona headed down the wooden walkway to the sandy area.

Her cousin followed, being the courteous one to offer greetings to the various passersby.

"Let's sit over here." Fiona found a large tree trunk that would suffice as a bench. She dusted off most of the sand and took a seat, scooting over for Belinda.

"All right. Not that I had anything to do, but why are we sitting out here like the world is about to come crashing down?"

"When you put it like that, it makes what I'm feeling sound shallow." Fiona didn't know how to read her own feelings.

"Sorry. But I'm in the dark. I'm not sure what emotion I should be feeling."

"I have a brother."

"You what? Get the hell out of here. When did this happen?"

Fiona filled her cousin in on the details. Belinda was too stunned to question her as she relayed the chronology of events.

"But that's not the only reason we're out here. So talk to me."

"I'm angry."

"With…?"

"Don't be difficult. My mother."

"I want to be clear because this is a situation that isn't quite clear. Are you angry that your mother didn't tell you? But can you understand why?"

"Don't sit there taking her side."

Belinda put her arm around Fiona's shoulder and pulled her into a big hug. "You want to punch something?"

Fiona glared at Belinda.

"Or do you want to celebrate?"

"What?" Fiona wasn't in the mood for taking the higher ground.

"Who's suffering more, you or Aunt Verona? Who has to live with her decision, you or Aunt Verona? Who will be ripped apart in the media, you or Aunt Verona?"

"Oh, stop talking."

"No, I won't stop talking until I shove some sense into that thick head and under that thin skin of yours. You can be the supportive, strong person for your mother and father. They will need that fierce, independent attitude when things get overwhelming."

"Would you be upset? Don't make it sound like I'm feeling something out of the ordinary."

Belinda didn't answer right away. She stared out at the water, her eyes focused on a distant boat with its white sails. "Honestly, I don't know. But I don't want you to implode over the situation. Nothing has changed in your life. You have a brother out there, but your life with your parents doesn't have to change. You are in control of how you react. That much I do know."

Fiona drew up her legs to rest her chin on her knees.

Control remained the elusive element to anchor her emotions.

"Why do you figure that I shouldn't have any feeling about this situation? My mother? This man?"

"That's not what I was saying. Of course you have emotions. You're human. But what you are angry about is not knowing earlier, not being in on the decision that your mom had to make, not being the one to decide that using Leo to find your brother and not tell you was a good idea. All out of your control."

"I figured out who I want to punch." Fiona glowered at her cousin, who held her smug smile in place.

"You can thank me later."

Fiona groaned. "I left my mother in the sitting room."

"Like you walked out and left?"

"Yep. And I wasn't understanding and definitely not supportive."

"Aunt Verona is a tough cookie. But I'm sure she'd appreciate hearing a change of heart from you. Remember, Grace kind of pushed this to the front. That had to be a lot of pressure on your mom."

"I know who's helping to uncover the secret, but I wonder who helped in keeping it."

"Why? So you can get worked up again?"

Fiona thought about her comment. "Yeah."

Belinda stood and extended a helping hand. "Let's go. You can't hide out here. I'm sure that your mother is really worried. If she goes to Grace to tell her that you ran off, then the entire household will be forming a search party. You didn't leave under normal circumstances." Belinda wiggled her fingers since Fiona hadn't acted on the cue. "You know that we are a high-maintenance bunch."

Finally, Fiona took her cousin's hand. "We can go now. But I thought that I'd be drinking."

"You didn't need your brain all muddled while I dropped my wisdom on you."

"Growing up sucks." Fiona brushed the sand off her behind.

"Not all the time. You've got a lot to be thankful for, especially with Leo in the picture."

"Don't even try to segue into my personal business. We are not talking about Leo." Fiona playfully side-bumped her on the way back to the car.

They laughed and started the drive back to the estate with a much lighter frame of mind. To think that this was supposed to be another family vacation. Maybe if she'd had an inkling of this news, she wouldn't have shown up.

"When are you heading back toward Midway?" Belinda asked. They had a deal for Fiona to drive her back home.

"I was planning to drive back on Saturday or Sunday. What's up?"

"Got to get back to work on Friday. Jesse set up an important meeting and would like me to be there. He's not completely comfortable with business terminology." Belinda looked hopeful.

"Friday, as in tomorrow?"

Belinda nodded. "It's not like you're going to miss anything here. My parents are gone. Dana skipped town soon after she got here. Pretty soon it'll be Aunt Cassie, Grandpa Henry and Grace only. Not exactly three of the partying type of people."

But Fiona wasn't thinking of them. She planned to have a kick-butt send-off with Leo. The type of farewell that was full of X-rated fun.

"Wipe the silly grin off your face. I know you're thinking about Leo. It's not like you all are ending here. You told me that you were going official as boyfriend-girlfriend. Have him meet you at your place on Friday."

"I don't know if he's done with Grace. Just because I was brought into the loop doesn't mean that his part is done."

"So ask him. It's not breaking confidences to tell you if he can leave on Friday. Besides, if you do leave, then you don't look so desperate."

"And you get what you want," Fiona countered.

"Do this, and then you don't owe me for my counseling session."

"Oh, gee, really? Thank you," Fiona mocked. But she knew that by tomorrow, she'd be heading upstate.

Leaving the estate was a significant step toward reality. Since she'd arrived, the place had taken on a magical quality that she didn't understand. The family was going to be stronger because of this information. She was happier. And even though her mother was facing hurdles, she could breathe a little easier that she didn't have to hold on to a secret.

They pulled up at the garage and Fiona was out of the car the second Belinda turned off the engine.

"Just be ready to go by six in the morning. I want to get through the city before rush hour," Fiona tossed over her shoulder.

"Then make it five."

Fiona groaned but nodded. She looked at her watch and figured that Leo was done working for the day. Besides, she had unfinished business with her mom. "Thanks, Belinda. Love you lots, cuz."

"You, too. Don't be hard on yourself. And don't be hard on your mom."

Fiona waved as she headed off to search for her mother. Then she wanted to talk to Grace. And then she had to finish up her questions for Leo. He had major explaining to do. Neither his big, sexy eyes nor his crisp, smooth voice could sway her from the anger nestled in her core. She had wrecked his trust. Now he'd taken his turn to blast hers to smithereens. What raised her annoyance was the blindsiding. Leo had given nothing away, even as they'd showed their vulnerabilities to each other. This matter went beyond attorney-client privilege privilege. This was her life.

Chapter 10

Leo looked at the third envelope that had been returned unopened with Addressee Unknown stamped across the front. An envelope had been sent every week to Dresden since Leo's return from the Hamptons. They'd found an email address, which they used with a less detailed plea. Grace was ready whenever they got Dresden's address to pull up in her car and personally knock on the man's door. Leo resisted that route, preferring to play by Dresden's rules and his timetable. And if there was no happy ending to the story, Leo was ready to break that news to Grace.

He closed the file on his desk as someone knocked on his door.

"Leo, Mrs. Meadows is here to see you."

"Thanks, Lucia. Please show her to my office."

Fiona popped in with a big smile. "I love your shocked expression."

"I thought you were Grace. My secretary said 'Mrs. Meadows.'"

"I know. I lied. Wanted to see how much you're at attention when my grandmother is yanking your chain."

"And…?" He opened his arms, inviting her to evaluate him.

"You look very casual."

He nodded.

"Guess you all are practically buds now."

"You can say that."

"I do say that. She's been harping on me about how wonderful you are. That you are a keeper."

"I'm glad her conversation with you is consistent with her conversation with me." Here they were back again, on the surface of the frozen pond. One false step and he'd be down and pulled by unseen currents. Despite the promises to head into part two of their relationship, Leo realized that Fiona stayed far away from any movement toward a real exchange of intimacy. He was trying his hardest to understand and go with the flow.

"I don't disagree with any of it."

"Even that I'm a keeper."

"Especially."

"For the record, she says that you're a keeper, too."

Fiona tilted her head and studied him. "She wouldn't use those words."

"Busted. But it's the thought that counts." Why did she have to dress as a sexy librarian, with black thick-framed glasses as a sweet touch?

"My grandmother would say that I'm a handful."

Leo nodded, agreeing wholeheartedly with the sentiment. "I appreciate you popping over, but how can I help you?"

She unfastened the top button of her starched white shirt. "We used to have our lunch treats. I don't know about you, but I miss it a lot."

He came around from behind his desk and buttoned her shirt and walked back to his seat. "That was the Hamptons."

She unpinned the bun in her hair. "Location doesn't affect my appetite."

He moved papers from one side of the desk to the other. If he didn't, he'd run his hand through her hair, clutch a handful and bring her halfway across the desk for a kiss.

"And this desk is the perfect width." She dragged her finger over the surface. "And the perfect length. Like a certain body part I know." She puckered her lips.

Damn. He was hard.

"I can't. My secretary may come in."

"No, she won't. I told her that I didn't want to be disturbed for about twenty minutes." She crossed her legs. "It's all clear."

Leo sat back in his chair. His woman was unbelievable. And she was making it difficult to say no to the temptation.

She scooted over the surface of the desk until she was in front of him. She slowly slid her legs open. "Commando," she mouthed.

His phone buzzed. He took a deep breath and checked the incoming message.

Ready to talk.

Leo sat forward. *Dresden.* "Fiona, I'm going to have to get with you a little later. I have to take this." He waved the phone.

She pouted but didn't move.

He kissed the tip of her nose, but his focus was on contacting Dresden before the man refused to take his calls. "Scoot. I have got to get to work."

"Remember this. When you come to my office to get down and dirty, I'll give you the brush-off."

"You have a cubicle." He winked.

"And that makes it a sweeter challenge." She adjusted her clothing, leaving her hair to fall onto her shoulders, and exited his office with a delicious sway to her hips.

"Well, ladies, on a weeknight, we're here. It's time to go see what our grandmother wants." Fiona was the first to get to the door. Dana and Belinda followed, fussing about the scheduled family meeting at their grandparents' upstate New York home.

The door opened and Mrs. Finch popped into view.

"Mrs. Finch, I didn't expect to see you here." Fiona hugged the house manager and waited for her cousins to get through their greetings.

"I'll be working over this way for a bit until after the birthday celebration."

"That's good news for us because we are over our heads with this stuff," Dana admitted before Fiona could offer a similar confession.

"Let's get together after the meeting tonight and clear up a few details for the birthday," Belinda said.

"Sounds good, ladies. Well, go on into the living room. Everyone is here."

Fiona again led the way to the living area. She made the rounds exchanging hellos.

"As you know, we've been trying to reach out to Dresden. Good news is that he responded to my letter."

"Great!" Fiona exclaimed louder than anyone else. "So when do we meet him?"

"He's only meeting with Leo." Grace raised her hand to squelch the chatter. "I don't want to overwhelm the young man. But since that's a go, the next thing that I want to discuss is having him there at the birthday party."

"Awkward, Grandma." Dana shook her head. "Do you plan to include him in the family video montage?"

"You can't," Verona shook her head, too. Her panicked expression was available for all to see. "The guests...they don't know."

"Why don't we make a public statement before the birthday in the spirit of family togetherness?" Fiona suggested.

"Can't. Or rather, we won't do that without Dresden's permission. I want to be as sensitive as possible, although I dearly want to do whatever it takes for him to be at the birthday celebration." Grace sat next to Verona. Their obvious unity over the matter showed in Verona's hand in Grace's.

"How do we know what he's going to do?" Dana looked around the room. Naturally, every member of the family was there.

"Leo is heading off to see Dresden this evening." Verona shared the news.

"Where is that?"

"Canada. Toronto."

Fiona nodded at each revelation, pretending that she knew that Leo was gone and what his destination was.

"When does Leo get back?" Belinda asked the question, her attention bouncing between Grace and Fiona.

"Don't know yet. He was on his way to the airport about an hour ago. Fiona, did he give you any further details?"

She shook her head. Further details? He hadn't told her one thing about it, nor about going on a flight.

"I would also like to announce the expansion of the family foundation's focus to include single parents. In the meantime, let's put our heads together to come up with a few organizations for consideration. And I want my daughters to run the foundation."

Silence descended like a two-ton boulder. Grace had always touted her granddaughters as the keepers of the legacy and continuation of Meadows Media's success. They certainly didn't need an additional task on their plates.

Fiona clapped, cheering on the grand gesture toward her mother and aunts. They were not left out or seen as no longer relevant. Although her mother had never shared those thoughts, the general feeling from the outside was that Grace had faith in only her granddaughters. Before long, the others were also cheering and hugging over the news.

"All right, enough of that. We've got work to do," Grace said.

"Could you excuse me for one sec?" Fiona headed out of the room and aimed for the library. She needed privacy to make her call. The phone rang, but Leo didn't answer. She let it go to voice mail to leave a message, except her phone beeped with an incoming call.

"Leo? Why didn't you tell me that you had talked to Dresden? And that you were going to Toronto. I had to find out from my grandmother in front of everyone. And they think that I know what's going on. But I didn't know squat." She stopped, as her frustration petered out.

"Let's talk when I get back," he said. The background noise from wherever he was interjected itself.

"No. I want to talk now."

"I didn't have time to tell you that I was leaving for Toronto. Dresden had changed his mind and I didn't want to give him time to pull back the offer."

"But you didn't tell me that you'd been in touch at all."

"I'm still working for Grace. The fact that you were brought up to date came from your mother and Grace. But I still have my original assignment, which I was hired to do."

"But you know how important this is to me."

"And you know how important my job is to me." He sighed. "Look, I'm sorry that you feel left out of the picture. We'll talk more when I get back."

"Sorry for jumping down your throat. Have a safe trip." Fiona hung up the phone and exhaled.

She doubted that they would talk about it to her satisfaction when he got home. Part of the unspoken issue was that she wanted a true partnership. Sometimes, she felt that they had gotten past their own hurdles, but then she could feel him retreating or her wanting to leap forward. The mistiming scared her; she worried that they weren't in sync and might not ever be the right fit.

A knock on the door broke her out of her reverie.

Her mother entered and hovered close enough to

touch her. "Hey, I was checking to see if you're okay. You looked upset."

"It's nothing. I had to talk to Leo."

"Everything okay?" Her mother's concern moved her.

"Yeah. We're still working out some kinks."

Verona rubbed her arm. "There will always be kinks. And that's the beauty of falling in love."

"Mom…"

"You don't think that you're in love? Please. It's all over your face when you're with him, when you're thinking about him and when you think it's not going right. Both of you are playing musical chairs with that one chair that might leave one of you standing because you're not thinking about the other. You're both very much in your own heads, as if it's a game that only one can win." Verona walked back to the door. "Now, come on. We've got a birthday to plan."

Leo sat in the hotel lobby, feeling anything but in control. This job wasn't about his success. After all, he'd found Grace's grandson and now had managed to make contact. The rest of this unique situation was about making Fiona happy, and he knew that part of the equation involved meeting her brother. Something that he should have made happen much earlier.

"Mr. Starks." Dresden approached from behind and moved into view.

Leo stood—otherwise, he'd have had to crane his neck to get the full view of Dresden. "Call me Leo, please."

They sat in the corner of the lobby. Not much foot traffic on a midweek afternoon in the area. Although he was in Canada, Leo knew all he'd see would be departing and arriving flights, due to the hotel's proximity to the airport.

"I'm glad that you agreed to meet me." Leo opted to start the conversation.

"I didn't think that I had a choice, since you weren't going to stop sending the letters."

Leo failed to hide his surprise. So he had gotten the letters. "Grace is desperate to open conversation."

At the mention of her name, Dresden's mouth tightened.

"Who are you to the family? Are you one of the sons or grandsons?"

"I'm a lawyer, one of many who work with the family." No need to mention his ties to Fiona. Too much suspicion already brewed in Dresden's demeanor. "We wanted to handle the meeting as delicately as possible and according to your wishes."

"Aren't they afraid of me blabbing about being the lost, abandoned child?"

"Grace would love to share the news with everyone. Her birthday celebration is next month and she's hoping that you agree to be there."

"To be brought before the queen. What about her daughter?"

"Your mother… Verona…would like to meet you, too."

"That's not happening." Dresden's hands clenched on the ends of the armrest. "As a matter of fact, none of it is happening. I came out of curiosity. Nothing more."

Leo didn't push. How could he, when the situation demanded understanding and patience? Dresden deserved respect for his own feelings.

"Does Verona have other kids?"

"A daughter…Fiona."

Dresden nodded. "And she knows?"

"Only recently. She really would like to meet you."

"Why? To convince me to meet her mother?"

Leo couldn't know what was on Fiona's mind, but he knew that her desire to meet Dresden had more to do with her own emotions than the desire to be a cheerleader on her mother's behalf. "She is her own woman."

"Look, I'm glad that I met you. I'm still not sure about the family. But I won't close the door on ever meeting them."

"That's all I can ask of you. I'm here until tomorrow. If you'd like to meet or ask me any questions, I'm here."

"Thanks." Dresden stood, shook his hand and left.

One thing that Leo noticed was that Dresden didn't waffle with indecision. But in this case, he hoped that tonight Dresden would be overcome with some level of curiosity, if not deeper emotions, and agree to meet again. He liked the man on paper. Meeting him in person didn't change his initial judgment. And he was sure that Grace and the rest of the family would rally around him. As for Fiona, she did deserve to meet, if not bond, with her brother. He hoped that within the next twenty-four hours, Dresden would reach out and see him again before he returned to New York.

Chapter 11

Another missing-persons case added to the pile. Fiona walked out of the department briefing hoping that this case would have a happy ending. While some cases involved criminal mischief, this particular one was about life's sad realities. An elderly man suffering from dementia had wandered off from the family home the previous night. A multidepartmental task force would get busy with a search of the area. Every minute was critical.

"Hey, Fiona, someone is here to see you." Jacinda popped her head into the cubicle.

"Family member?" She looked at her watch. No meetings were set up until later that morning.

"Nah. Good-looking dude, though." Jacinda winked at her. "I thought you were all lovey-dovey with Lawyer Man."

"Where's he at?" Fiona wanted to cut off Jacinda's probing of her personal life.

"Down the hall in the meeting room. I'll be rolling out in a half hour if you want to ride with me."

"Cool. Come get me if I'm not done. I wasn't expecting anyone. Shouldn't take long."

Jacinda gave her a thumbs-up and left.

Fiona couldn't imagine who was here to see her. But she had a full day ahead of her. No time for personal visits from a possible former boyfriend. She pushed open the conference room door, now curious to see her visitor.

"Fiona, good morning."

"Dresden? What are you doing here?" Fiona was more than a little flustered to see her brother.

Shock slowed down her brain function. First, her family had never shown up at her workplace. Just as most people avoided voluntarily visiting the hospital, her cousins preferred to steer clear of the police precinct. Besides, her personal life and work life didn't mix. In order to maintain her sanity for what she had to do in her job, she kept her worlds separate. Now Dresden had shown up looking upset and eager to talk to her.

"Coffee?" Fiona asked.

"No. I've been in town for a few days. I'm flying out at noon. But I wanted to talk to you."

"Okay, have a seat." His unease sparked a similar reaction in her.

She didn't outwardly show surprise that he had been in town and hadn't contacted her, keeping her disappointment to herself. He didn't owe her anything.

Fiona needed to hear what he wanted, but she also

didn't have a lot of time to wait for him to reveal why he was there. She cleared her throat, which seemed to snap his attention back to the present.

"Grace's letter started it all. I read it almost every day." He rested his hands on the table. His gaze aimed downward on his fingers. "And it says everything that I wanted it to say when I found out that I was adopted. My parents didn't hide it from me."

Fiona nodded. She didn't want to interrupt him now that he'd shared this information.

"But in that letter, she says that she wants to meet me. The family wants to meet me." His fingers curled in. His mouth tightened. She guessed that it was anger. "The Meadows family wants to meet me."

"Yes, we all do. I was lucky enough to meet you. I appreciate that you allowed it."

"Why wouldn't I? Yeah, it took almost a month after getting the emails from Leo, but I had to work through a few things." He looked at her and she felt as if she were looking in a mirror. The roundish shape of their eyes matched. "We have the same mother. Besides, Leo had said how special it would be to meet you." Dresden nodded. "He was right. It was special."

"Looks like I have Leo to thank, then." She tucked Leo's consideration to her heart.

"But I can't meet the rest. I don't want to. Leo told me to think about it. I guess Grace must have pushed him to get an answer from me. But I can't." He shook his head. "I'm not ready."

"You don't have to do anything that you don't want to. I hope you're not feeling pressured to meet the family."

Dresden shrugged. "I know they will be disappointed. Leo told me that he hadn't gone back to his village in Brazil after he was adopted."

"But your reluctance is understandable because it was from birth." She didn't mean to have an outburst. This personal conversation between Leo and him unsettled her, made her question why she wasn't Leo's confidante.

"Love is a strange thing, though. How does loving someone depend on how you were loved?"

"What did you say?" Fiona sensed that this conversation was turning into an analysis of Leo and her. The tenet sounded too familiar, too similar to the source of conflict that arose frequently between her and Leo.

"I hope Leo wouldn't let fear dictate his relationship with you."

"I don't know what to say." She really didn't know.

"I know he's a busy man and I left him a message. But I wanted to say that it was nice meeting you, Fiona." Dresden stood.

Numb and confused, she also pushed back her chair and stood. "Thanks for coming in, Dresden. Whenever you're ready to meet, I'm here and the family is here."

He nodded and left the room.

Fiona stayed put, reeling from the sudden loss that she felt as her brother walked out of her life. She wanted to run after him and beg him to stay, give them all a chance. But his reluctance was understandable. Hopefully, time could heal all wounds. Hopefully, Grace's letter would continue to be the inspiration that brought Dresden back into the fold.

"Yo, Fiona, we've got to roll." Jacinda jingled her keys.

"Let's go find Mr. Lowenstein." Fiona did the mental switch back to her work. Everything imploding in her personal life would have to wait.

A day in the Hamptons sounded like the perfect escape. Ever since Leo returned to the office, his workload had increased as a measure of his success with the Meadows portfolio. A dozen new cases had landed on top of his already overstuffed client inbox.

His day began before the rest of the staff came in and he didn't leave until late in the evening. A couple nights, he'd actually slept on the couch in his office because the team was working on a time-sensitive deal. His condo felt like a vacation home and the office served as the home front. No sense in whining. He had career aspirations and had to do the groundwork to get to the next level.

That excuse worked on him, but it wasn't going over well with Fiona. They barely saw each other. A nugget of doubt made him question whether it was deliberate on her end. He wasn't a saint, canceling their nights out or falling asleep in her arms. But their conversations would drift off to inconsequential chats with the obligatory *Talk to you later*. The whole thing frustrated him, showing him that trying to hold on to it all—career and relationship—promised to be difficult. He feared that it might be impossible.

Something had gotten disconnected between him and Fiona. It wasn't his imagination that she'd emotionally drifted, setting sail without him. She didn't grumble. She didn't demand her time with him. As a matter of fact, she accepted his excuses and went on her way.

Yet it didn't prevent him from missing the hell out of Fiona. A few phone messages seemed to be all they could manage with each other. Their brief actual conversations were turning stilted. Something that he couldn't put his finger on was off. But the unease had to stay off to the side for the busy upswing of his career. Now the goal he'd wanted was at his fingertips. The buzz around the office suggested that a big shakeup was about to take place at Grayson, Buckley and Tynesdale.

"Hey, Leo, the Hasbergers have signed on for us to handle their family trust." Timothy Grayson updated him with the good news.

"Congratulations. I know that was a big win."

"Yeah. Took some maneuvering, let me tell you." His boss looked quite pleased with himself. But he should, since the family's net worth was $3 billion. "So looks like we'll need you to head to the city tonight. Big meeting early in the morning."

Leo's heart sank. His first normal day in a while, and he wanted to surprise Fiona with a night out.

"Is there a problem?"

"No. Not at all."

"The jet will take you at seven o'clock. Works for you?"

Leo nodded. His mind raced at possibilities to salvage his plans and get his work done. He picked up the phone and made a few calls to arrange his surprise. Then he dialed Fiona.

"Hey, late night at work?" she asked.

"Actually, no. I'm free for the night and I want to hang out with you."

She giggled. "Okay, coming over?"

"Only to pick you up. We're heading to New York City."

"What? It's Thursday night. It'll take forever to get there and then I have to head back for work."

"I'll take less than two hours in the jet."

"Did you say *jet*?"

"Uh-huh. And…we'll eat, have hot naked sex and then sleep it off. Call in tomorrow. Or I can get the jet to take you back."

"You're so tempting me right now."

"You and me, baby." He paused to drum up the courage to say what was on his mind. "And we can talk. I know things have been rough with my schedule."

"I've been busy, too."

"But I don't want us to get used to not being together. You know what I mean."

"Yeah. I know. We should talk."

The fact that she easily agreed heightened his nervousness.

"Okay, I'll be there around six. Bye, babe. Love ya."

"Yeah, me, too."

He hung up and sat back in his chair. "This is not good. Not good at all."

Leo did his best to shake off the doom-and-gloom vibes. His lady deserved the best night on the town. They used to enjoy their impromptu drives when they were in the Hamptons and it felt good to escape and release themselves from the family drama. With the extravagant plans he had under way, Fiona would have a fun and decadently wicked night. To get ready for the part, he shaved, showered and then dressed in his black Tom Ford suit. Surveying himself in the mirror, he liked the classic simplicity of the tailored suit with its sleek lines. Not one for fashion trends, he wanted to look the role of the playboy this time. He couldn't wait to see Fiona's reaction to her Brazilian nerd.

The limo arrived on time to pick him up and then they were on their way for Fiona. He'd texted her that she should dress like a Connecticut socialite. She'd responded with a smiley face and told him that he wouldn't be disappointed.

"Sir, we're here." The driver held open his door.

Leo exited. Suddenly he felt like a guy at his prom. The door opened and Fiona stepped out in a red dress that fit like a sheath, stopping midthigh to show off her legs in matching fashionable shoes. "Wow."

She stepped into his chest and kissed him softly on his cheek. She rubbed off the lipstick imprint she left. He noted that she was eye to eye with him in her sexy shoes. "You, my darling, are looking fantastic. The suit makes me want to do all kinds of nasty with you."

"I'm channeling my inner Double-O spy and picked the same clothing designer."

"Smart move. I'm looking forward to giving up my secrets to your charm."

They got back into the limo and headed for the airport. By seven o'clock, they were in the air on their way to New York City. So far, the plans were unfolding as he'd hoped. He poured a glass of wine for her. "To us."

"Hear, hear." She sipped her wine and smacked her lips in appreciation. "This is good."

"Sauvignon blanc."

"I'll leave it to you to know the details." She kicked off her shoes and placed her feet on his lap. "It feels good to have you to myself. It's been a while."

He rubbed his hand along her legs. Touching her

was a trigger. She sensed his discomfort and didn't help matters by brushing her foot against his arousal.

"Don't start nothin'." He loved how smoky her eyes were with browns and golds outlining her lids and brows. She looked like the temptress that he'd wanted and now had. "We'll be landing soon."

"Bummer. I was hoping to knock an item off my bucket list."

He planted a kiss on her inner ankle. "We'll be knocking off a few other things later tonight."

"Oh yeah?" She swung her legs off his lap and fixed her clothing. "Then I'll behave like a lady with proper decorum for the remainder of the ride." She drained her wineglass. "Had to guzzle that last bit." She set down the glass and smiled.

He wanted to kiss her so badly. Whatever shade of red painted her lips played with his determination to act like a gentleman and not kiss every bit off her mouth.

The plane began its descent in the nick of time.

"Ready for the night of your life?" He stood and extended his hand.

"Yes, Mr. Starks. Are you ready for the night of your life?" She winked at him and, for an added touch, licked the plump surface of her lips.

Leo escorted her out of the plane. The wind had a bite to it and they both had to button their coats. They hurried to the car and gratefully got in.

"Mr. Starks, there has been a change of plans. Mr. Grayson has asked that you come to the office."

"Excuse me? No, I've got dinner reservations. I'm meeting Mr. Grayson tomorrow."

"I understand, sir." The driver repeated his statement with the same slow dryness that couldn't be misunderstood.

"It's okay, Leo." Fiona placed her hand over his. He hoped it was a sign of her support. Because this wasn't the night he'd planned.

"Fine. Let's go." Leo tried to make small talk for the rest of the trip. But he was a man, plain and simple. "One night. That's all I wanted."

"Shhh. You can rant later." Fiona tilted her head toward the driver.

Leo didn't care if he was heard. He exhaled his frustration. Yes, he did care.

They pulled up in front of the massive office building on West 52nd Street. Its dominance took over the block. He'd been there only a handful of times, with the smaller upstate office handling mostly Meadows business and a few other wealthy clients in the area. Any other time, like tomorrow, he'd have been happy to hop out and let the world know that he was a lawyer for the firm.

"Go see what they want and then I'll have you to myself later," Fiona urged.

"Where are you going?"

"You booked a hotel room, right?"

"Yeah." He dug inside his jacket pocket. "Here is the key card. St. Regis."

"Oooh, fancy." She plucked the key out of his hand, leaned over and popped him a kiss. "Now get out and let me go play in our room."

"Suite," he corrected. "Tiffany Suite."

Fiona giggled. "Mr. Starks, I just might slide you over to the keeper side." She slipped her hand between his legs and squeezed. "Now go on and be a good lawyer."

Her chuckle and good-luck squeeze boosted his energy to charge into the building. After showing the necessary ID and badge, he got on the elevators and headed for the top floor. Grayson had better have a good reason to block him from his date night. The doors swooshed open and Leo pasted on his confident grin.

"Mr. Starks, good to see you… Oh, you look…very fine."

"Thank you. I had plans for the evening. Was there an emergency?"

"Sorry for the interruption. But I wanted to share my announcement with you." He beckoned him to enter fully into the room. "And also share it among the partners."

Leo looked to the cluster of women and men standing with serious countenances. Was this some sick ritual before he got fired? He looked at Grayson for an explanation but dreaded what he was about to say.

"We have decided to offer you partnership. Your peers have unanimously voted for your inclusion. I hope you will accept."

"Yes." Leo wanted to take a seat. Have a drink. Call Fiona.

"Great. The finer details will be discussed tomorrow and press releases will be sent out. But this couldn't wait. The partners wanted to surprise you with their decision but also tell you right away."

The applause and cheers continued while Grayson spoke to him. He could barely catch all the details, but he figured whatever he didn't hear, he could follow up on the next day.

"Champagne for everyone." One of the other senior partners and founders, Buckley, stepped forward and motioned for the bottles to be brought into the room.

Leo spent the next couple of hours sipping on champagne and getting to know the partners. He knew that he'd jumped over the senior associate position. The leap wasn't a bad thing. The unofficial gossip was that the senior associates were the lawyers who were consistent in their jobs but not exceptionally aggressive with acquiring new cases. They were also content with not ever becoming partner. Truthfully, he'd worried that he would fall into that category and have his career aspirations stunted before they got a chance to develop.

One thing was clear about the partners: they could drink. Empty champagne bottles were stacking up at a significant rate. But even though moods were upbeat thanks to the bubbles, business didn't go to the back burner. The partners were in full conversation about their clients. As he glanced at his watch, he wondered how one broke away from the pack.

"Mr. Grayson, would you need me to stick around longer?" His wish to depart his promotion celebration could be counted as a ding against him, but he wanted to be with Fiona.

"Yes. We're not done. Apparently, the Hasbergers wanted to come and join in the celebration. I thought it a wonderful bonus. And then tomorrow we can start working on the trust." He looked at his wrist. "They should be here any minute."

Leo nodded. He needed to call Fiona.

"Leo, congratulations. Look, we must get out on the golf course."

"Thanks, Mr. Tynesdale, but I don't play golf."

"Don't or can't?"

"I can play—I don't."

"Then we've got to fire up that desire. Let's get out there this weekend. We can hit the golf course in Sawgrass." Tynesdale flashed his toothy grin and then his massive diamond ring as he tossed back his champagne.

The weekends used to be the catch-up days for his personal life. Slowly, they had turned into the travel days to get to meetings. Flying in and out of airports to get to appointments with clients. Anytime he did manage to stay at home, he was too exhausted to be any good.

"Tynesdale, give the man time to breathe. Don't mind him, Leo. He's a fanatical golf enthusiast." Buckley guided Tynesdale off to another cluster of partners.

It was almost eleven o'clock. Leo took the opportunity to find an empty office where he could call Fiona. His night was turning into a bittersweet event. He dialed the number and waited, wondering if he should share his news first to soften her up or jump right in and deal with her anger. If he were in her shoes, he would not be a happy man. He left a message that he should be there in a couple of hours.

"Leo, there you are. The Hasbergers are here." Grayson waited at the door. He wore his grin like a proud mentor showing off an apt pupil.

"Would love to meet them." Leo placed the phone back into his pocket, along with his fears that while his life was in the takeoff position in one area, there was high potential for a crash landing in another.

Later that night, at the Tiffany Suite in the St. Regis, Leo opened the door. Lights were on. Classical music played softly over the speakers. What might have been a romantic tune sounded more like a mournful march as he aimed for the bedroom.

He'd picked the St. Regis for its prominent mark on the early 1900s New York landscape, courtesy of its wealthy builder, John Jacob Astor IV. But now that history and all of the room's aesthetic features—trademark Tiffany-blue walls, the chandelier with its cascading pearls, the private fireplace—faded into the background.

He opened the bedroom door and looked in on Fiona curled up under the covers. He picked up the red dress that lay on the edge of the bed. Her shoes were not far away on the floor. Her scent lingered around the room, a reminder of what he'd missed.

Leo undressed as quietly as he could and slipped under the covers to spoon her. She felt so good against his body, more than warmth, but something solid to hold on to in his life. He rested his forehead against her head, sighing as he burrowed into the silky softness of her hair. Nothing could replace this feeling of having his woman in his arms. Whatever was trying to stir between them, whatever was trying to pry them apart, couldn't happen without a fight.

Fiona awoke to the sound of the shower. She squinted, trying to focus her sleepy, confused mind to figure out where she was.

New York City.

She yawned and hugged one of the many pillows in the luxurious bed. The elegant furniture made her feel like a princess. Too bad her prince ditched her last night. And now he was singing a Bruno Mars song. She checked her phone for messages and noticed that he'd called. By the time of his call, she'd already downed a couple glasses of wine, eaten a scrumptious steak dinner and gorged on a decadently sweet chocolate cake before peeling off her dress and crashing in the bed.

She just wanted to barge in and confront Leo but was too lazy to get out of the bed. Hopefully, they would get a chance for a redo today. She had nothing planned for the weekend: maybe they could extend their getaway for another night. Satisfied with that fix, she waited for him to exit the bathroom.

When he did emerge, she expected that he'd have a towel wrapped around his hips or, for her pleasure, be completely naked. Instead he was already dressed, looking shiny and so damn sexy. Now she had to stamp down her rising desire.

"What the hell? It's only seven o'clock in the morning. Your office is across town." She waved her hand, feeling directionally challenged in this luxury suite that did a good job of blocking out the world.

"I got a promotion."

Why did he have to smile? She was too damn weak for her own good.

"I'm a partner. Can you believe that?"

"Yes, I can. You work your butt off." She gave his behind an appreciative smack. "At least there's still some left for me to enjoy." She kissed him. "Congratulations. So when can we celebrate?"

"I'm heading to Connecticut today. Then tonight I'm heading with the Hasbergers to their private island in the British Virgin Islands."

"Uh-huh." She waited to hear when she'd fit into this suddenly exclusive schedule. He smiled at her again, and it would normally have knocked her off her feet. Right now, however, she was feeling a little salty over the entire situation.

"I know we had plans." He tilted her chin up and kissed the tip of her nose. "We'll get through this."

"I thought you wanted to have a talk."

"I do, but obviously not right now."

"Who do I contact to get on your schedule?"

"Don't pick a fight. I didn't know that I was getting the promotion or I would have left you home."

"*Left me home?* Wow, that's rich. It's always been about the promotion." Fiona deliberately didn't present her opinion as a question. "You the man now, right?"

"You want to judge me for my aspirations? I don't get to see you, either, because you're working your butt off on your job. Is that out of the goodness of your heart? Or is it also for a promotion?"

"Maybe we're not so different, where we want to bury ourselves into everything else but each other."

He waited for her to go on.

"Tell me I'm wrong. That you aren't just as afraid as I am to really feel, love, hope. That you don't worry about the uncertainty of life. That it doesn't choke you with fear. Tell me that you can surrender yourself, be vulnerable, all the things that you want from me."

"That sounds like you, not me."

Her eyes widened in reaction. "I'm sorry that I surrendered to the idea that I could do this...with you."

"What the hell are you saying?"

"Should we be together, two people too afraid to love unconditionally?" Fiona felt as if she'd boarded a runaway train and her fears were pouring out of her with the same loss of control.

"You're saying that nothing we've had mattered. What about our two weeks in the Hamptons?"

"What about the months after the Hamptons? You went back to being cool and emotionally unattainable."

He held her chin. "So according to you, we're two scared people."

She pushed him away. But only her body moved. He stood firm like a solid boulder.

"I came on the job without knowing that you'd be there. I kept business separate from pleasure. Is that why you're mad? Or are you so damn afraid of living that you find an excuse to screw up anything we have between us?" Leo let his frustration rush through the gate.

"Don't try to psychoanalyze me. You came into my family circle. Listened, judged and gave your two cents. But you stayed closed mouth about your life. I got a smattering of information, but you didn't open up. So don't try to rewrite history."

"You know what? Maybe you are right." He turned to leave. "I should play the game by your rules. Will that make you stay?" His back rose and fell as he paused at the doorway. Only his profile was visible.

"I'm not forcing you to live by my rules."

"Sure sounds like it." He walked away and out of the suite.

Fiona punched her fist in the pillow. Then she punched it over and over, until her arms were weary.

She had been looking for any reason to halt momentum. She wanted some time to pause and think. Now Leo had seen through her actions and was first to walk away, and from the sound of it, it was a permanent move.

Leo stood in the hallway, with his hand holding on to the door handle. He'd lost her. Again.

Chapter 12

The rain didn't hold back its fury, doling out punishment to add to Leo's misery. Water sloshed across the windshield, challenging the wipers to beat away the watery curtain for a clearer view. Mother Nature could throw her obstacles at him, but nothing would hold him from his goal—driving to Fiona's house outside of Essex County. However, he did have to ease onto the brakes a few times to keep the car solidly on the road. Oncoming headlights blinded him as he navigated the almost-emptied streets.

He could have waited until the next morning, but that meant precious hours to talk to Fiona lost. And it was his turn to ask and be granted a second chance. Once he'd made the decision, he was a man with a single focus.

The car lurched to a stop as he hit the brake hard.

Did the traffic light have to change now? He banged his hand against the steering wheel. There was no traffic in the intersecting street to trigger the light. One more hindrance designed to be a pain in his ass. Everything irritated him, testing the limits of his patience.

As soon as the traffic light turned green, the car pushed through the flooded streets. Of all the days for an hour-long deluge. This bad weather had the worst timing. The sucky situation wasn't helped by the fact that he'd already tried calling Fiona. No surprise that she didn't take his call. His accusations and judgments had successfully carved an impassable chasm, wide and deep, between him and her. That was why, close to midnight, he forged on through the city to get to her place with the blind hope that she'd be there. That she'd see him.

Just when the last drops of his patience had almost evaporated, he pulled up to her house. The windows were dark with drawn curtains. Only a single light shone over the front door. Leo noticed that the driveway was empty, but that fact didn't mean anything. Her car could be locked in the garage. Before his courage failed, he got out of the car. Within seconds, he was drenched. The cold November rain wasn't going to help him in his pursuit. He raised his jacket over his head and ran to the door. The meager cover did nothing to prevent the coldness and wetness.

Grateful for the small overhang above the doorway, he shook off the water and pushed the doorbell. It chimed through the house. No one answered. The house remained quiet and dark. No curtain pulled back; no footsteps sounded; no call floated out asking who was there.

Leo pulled out his phone and checked for any messages. Nothing. He dialed the one person whom he considered a friend to his plight.

"What's up, Leo? It's late." Belinda's worry was clear.

Leo hurried to defuse her concern. "I'm here. Outside Fiona's." He no longer thought that she was in the house, ignoring him.

"She's not home?"

"Doesn't look that way. I was hoping you could tell me if you knew where she might be." He didn't want to let on that he thought Fiona might be at her house. The cousins didn't hide their fierce allegiance to each other. And if they perceived him as the source of Fiona's unhappiness, then he could expect a complete shutout.

"She called Dana and me earlier today. Didn't say anything about going anywhere. We chatted about Grace's birthday party…after we talked about you."

Leo sucked in his breath. He didn't want to ask if he'd survived their analysis.

"I thought she was okay." Belinda offered him a crumb of hope that he gratefully took.

"Do you know if she'd have gone to Dana?" The youngest cousin initially hadn't been warm and fuzzy with him in the Hamptons. It wasn't until she saw Fiona genuinely happy that she'd relaxed her stance. They eventually had made their way to a place of mutual understanding.

Belinda tossed him more hope. "She's not at Dana's, because Kent came into town. I know that Fiona wouldn't want to encroach on their time. Maybe she's asleep."

"Maybe." Doubt lay heavy with his agreement. He looked up at the windows, which were still dark.

Fiona's cousin yawned. "I'll let you know if I hear from her."

"Thanks, Belinda." He couldn't ask for more. Nevertheless, he hung up, disappointed that nothing further could be accomplished. In one more attempt, he pounded on the door. "Fiona!"

A light popped on in the upstairs window of the house next door.

"Great. Next will be the police." Leo decided that it was time to give up and head back home. Luck wouldn't be on his side if he was caught by a vigilant neighborhood watch.

Soaked, cold and despondent, he got back into his car. But he didn't move, instead sitting in the driver's seat at the curb. At least the light in the neighbor's window had been turned off.

Looked like the rain had lessened its barrage. Time to figure out where to go and what to do next. Giving up wasn't in his DNA. He wanted to have his say and if Fiona couldn't forgive him, wouldn't accept his remorse, then he'd walk away knowing that he'd tried to earn her love.

In his final desperation, he opened the glove compartment and searched for a pen. Finding one, he dug around for anything that could serve as a note. An old electric-bill envelope provided the perfect solution. Water from his soaked head dripped onto the paper. Instead of using his lap, he moved the envelope onto the dashboard and used the surface as his desk. With the pen poised to write, he debated what tone to use, what words to write, how sentimental he should be. He quickly wrote what came to mind. "Fiona, let's talk. Please. Leo."

His stomach clenched as he retraced his path toward the house. Maybe he should have written "I love you." That could be too much. He didn't want to tip the scale to influence her feelings or make her think he was manipulating her.

With nothing to pin the note to the door, he opted to use a rock to anchor this important request. In front of the door, on the welcome mat, he left a part of his heart—a small ember of hope. Resignation over his failure settled in his gut on the ride home.

Fiona didn't know why she couldn't sleep. When she closed her eyes, the image of Leo's face came to mind. Every meaningful moment of their time spent together rolled like a movie with her as a spectator. But she didn't want to be outside the experience. And her heart was too sad to really dive in and relive those intimate hours spent in Leo's embrace.

Unwilling and unable to deal with the pain in her heart, she tossed aside the comforter and got out of bed and changed her clothes. Restless and hit with insomnia, she paced, going from room to room. The stormy night added its percussive beats against the roof, a suitable soundtrack for her dark mood.

Dressed in jeans and long-sleeved shirt, hair pulled into a messy ponytail and wearing ankle boots, Fiona felt like a soldier outfitted for battle. To move forward she'd have to push back, push aside the hurt that she clung to, afraid of believing that she deserved true happiness.

Talking to her brother—*hers*—her only sibling,

filled a hole that she hadn't known existed, much less known how to heal. While Leo had tried to do his part to help her, she'd deflected his advice. She'd turned away from what he offered, thinking that his comforting message made her that much weaker. Now her heart felt empty and sad. But spending time with Dresden, hearing his pain, sharing their views on so many things, even when they disagreed, were experiences that mattered.

And with such thoughts of her brother and Leo, her new emotions cascading into self-discovery, Fiona was ready. She picked up her keys, opened the door leading to the garage and got into the car. Her insecurities no longer had any power. Now she craved peace. Her heart and body knew just where to get it.

She hit the gas, and the tires squealed as the car reversed into the street. "Leo, I hope you're home." She blinked away the tears.

Insomnia had to be blamed for this crazy drive, close to midnight, in a major storm. Fiona gritted her teeth and cursed every time she hit a pothole. Maybe she should have phoned in her apology. She'd have done so now if she hadn't left her darn phone in her gym bag, now sitting in Dana's car. Her cousin was home with her honey. No way that they would answer their phones or care about hers.

She pulled up to Leo's condo property. Lucky for her, there was one car ahead, about to enter through the electronic gates. Closing the gap between her car and the one immediately in front, she practically piggybacked onto the sedan and got through the gates before they slid closed.

Her intent wasn't to launch a surprise invasion.

Since she hadn't gotten in touch with Leo in advance, her only option was to get on the other side of the massive gates by whatever creative means necessary.

The visitor space assigned to his condo was empty. *Good.* She didn't want to be the uninvited guest if Leo had company. Jealousy soured her stomach at the possible scenario of Leo and another woman spending the night together. Should she be offended, given the cold way she'd sent him off? *Hell yeah.*

Fiona stepped out of the car and into a deep puddle. Cold water covered her ankle boot. She cursed. Hair plastered to her face and against her neck, clothes turning into a second skin, Fiona didn't see the urgency to run toward the door. The damage had been done; her soaked clothing reminded her that she wasn't going to look her best if she did see him.

She took hold of the doorknocker and pounded away. She leaned back to survey the two-level unit, trying to discern any signs of movement. Placing her ear against the door, she listened, at the same time trying to block out the muffled sound of the rain beating against everything in its path.

"Please, Leo, if you're in there…please, I'm here." She whispered her plea over and over as she waited for any sounds indicating he was home. Her tears mixed with the rainwater that was already running down her cheeks.

As much as she'd begged him to come to the door, Fiona couldn't remain seated at the door in the pouring rain. She opted to take cover back in her car. Once out of the rain, she could think about her next move.

Sitting in her car did help her concentration somewhat. Her teeth chattered as the shivers racked her

entire body. She looked around the car for anything
to cover her. An extra jacket lay in the backseat. She
reached for it, grateful for the thin, dry layer. If conditions got too bad, she'd turn on the engine and the
seat warmer.

She leaned her head against the window and waited.
Faith that she was doing the right thing was what she
clung to for comfort. Her eyes grew tired with the vigilant watch. She rounded her shoulders to retain as much
warmth as possible. Time couldn't have moved any
slower. But she wasn't going anywhere. Determined
to stay, she snuggled down deeper into the seat, and
before long she fell asleep.

Leo scanned his resident card and passed through
the tall iron gates that slid open. He aimed the car toward his condo and pulled into his driveway.

"Could one thing go my way tonight?" He hit the
dashboard with his fist.

His anger was aimed at no one but himself. How
could he have been so stupid as to let Fiona out of his
life? *Again.* Sitting in his car wasn't going to bring her
back. Going inside wasn't going to do so, either. But
he was damp, cold and pissed off. A cursory glance
around the immediate area showed that he was the only
one outdoors at this time of night in the foul weather.

Leo frowned. Something nagged at his attention. He
twisted in his seat for a better look. This time he homed
his gaze on the cluster of cars parked in the designated
visitor spaces. There it was. He'd almost missed the
car. He blinked to ensure that it wasn't his imagination. There was the familiar SUV in his assigned visi-

tor parking space. He opened the window and stuck out his head. His focus was squarely on the driver.

"Fiona?" Leo jumped out of his car and ran over to hers. "Fiona!" His heart leaped at the realization. She'd been here while he wasted time standing around at her place. He knocked on the car window to rouse her, hoping it wasn't hard enough to startle her.

Finally, she stirred, but she did nothing more than snuggled deeper into her jacket.

"Fiona, wake up!" Now he didn't care how he woke her. Impatience won out. His fist pounded his desperation, not ceasing until her eyelids fluttered open.

As he'd feared, she awoke with a start. Through the closed window, he heard her muted scream. She looked around, then at him. Confusion accompanied her sleepy expression as she rubbed her eyes and yawned.

"Leo?" She flung open the door.

He had to jump out of the way to avoid her eager exit.

"You're home," she whispered. Her teeth chattered as she spoke. She wrapped her arms around herself and vigorously rubbed her arms. Wisps of her breath puffed outward with her exhalations.

"Come inside. You need to warm up. If you're not in a rush, you're welcome to toss your clothes in the dryer." He shoved his hands into his jeans to avoid the mistake of offering his body to warm hers.

"Thanks. Sounds like a plan." She followed him into the house.

"I'll get a robe for you while your clothes dry." Her hesitation made him add, "Should only take about forty-five minutes." Enough time for him to say what he needed to tell her.

She nodded. Standing in the living room with her arms still locked around body, she looked ready to walk out the door. He hurried to his room for the robe in case she did change her mind and leave.

He returned with the thickest robe, glad to see her still in his living room. She hadn't moved from her spot except to turn toward the window, where the drapes weren't drawn. The jacket still hung around her hunched shoulders. Her hair had lost its curl and bounce, but the effect hadn't dulled her natural beauty.

"Here you go." He held out the robe.

She turned and approached slowly, keeping her eyes on his gift. Her hands removed it from his grasp without touching him. He didn't miss the care she used not to make contact.

"You probably could use a cup of tea," His hospitality had a purely selfish motive. Whatever he could do to delay her departure, he would try. Most of all, he wanted her to feel comfortable. "You can change in the bathroom." He'd have suggested his bedroom, but the intimate space might not be seen in the best of light after their recent split.

As he spoke, she lifted her gaze to his face. A quiver of excitement rippled through him, supercharging his nerve endings. How could she not know that, with those beautiful big brown eyes, she wielded a power over him? His determination to not sweep her into his arms and kiss her until that signature giggle bubbled up barely held.

Every inch of him was aroused. Thinking about her was one thing. Standing this close, inhaling her soft perfume, feeling the energy from her close presence, rendered him hopelessly under her will. To stay grounded and pretend that he was emotionally disengaged, he clenched his jaws and looked away from scrutiny. For extra measure, Leo backed up, retreating from her. His primary goal was to not do anything that might set back this tentative meetup.

Fiona took the robe and gratefully pressed it to her body. She needed something to hold on to; otherwise, Leo would see how her hands trembled. The root cause of her condition wasn't the damp clothing. The warmth in the room had started to soothe her skin but couldn't calm the anxious pining of her emotions for the man who looked at her with such coldness.

"Hot tea sounds good." She hoped that it would take an eternity to sip her drink. She didn't want to leave but didn't know how to stay.

Except for backing away from her, he didn't move. Maybe he hadn't expected her to accept the offer of tea. Well, she'd given her answer and she wasn't going to make it easy for him to shut the door on her or them. Taking her time, she hugged the robe to her breast and ignored his direction to change in the bathroom. She went to the room that was once their sexual domain.

Leo noticed that Fiona didn't walk to the end of the hallway to the bathroom. Instead she stepped into his bedroom and closed the door. Her playful striptease skit was a thing of the past. No more peekaboo flashes of her breasts. No more sensual body waves as she poured honey down the valley of her breasts and over her abs. No more sexy hip wiggles as she slid her thong bikini down her legs. Damn, he was hard as hell.

Sex, and the memory of his good times with Fiona,

had to wait. More important than anything was the issuance of his apology. Once he had the chance to repair the damage, then maybe, just maybe, he could do more than linger over memories. They could re-create what they'd enjoyed and make new memories. But he was jumping ahead of himself.

So Leo turned his thoughts from past temptations and walked into the kitchen. For the next few minutes, he busied himself with the tea preparations. Remembering a client's gift, he opened the cabinet and pulled out a box of Scottish shortbread cookies.

"You don't have to do all of that. Just being in the warmth has helped a lot." Her voice softly touched him, as if a gentle stroke by her hand.

"It's no problem. I want to do this." Leo set the cup and plate of cookies on a serving tray. Once he was pleased with his presentation, he turned to address her. "Oh…" Thank goodness he didn't have the tray in his hand. "Whoa."

Fiona stood in the doorframe between the kitchen and dining area in her glorious natural nakedness.

While his mouth tripped up on monosyllabic words, every cell in his body roared to life. He felt like a once-sleeping giant awaking from a long slumber. Blood pumped through every vein. His arousal was no exception. He might have been coping before, but at this moment, he was alive.

Fiona's face glowed as if a special light lit her features. It was the full-watt bright smile that had reached out and ensnared his heart from the beginning. And now it was the smile that spoke where words were unnecessary to let him know that they would be all right.

"I'm dry now." She gave a short laugh. "Well, not

all of me." She bit her lip, a sexy habit that screwed with his self-control. "A special place is wet. *Very* wet for you. But otherwise, I'm warm and dry." Her hands rested on her hips and his gaze gladly followed the curves of its journey.

"How am I supposed to talk to you when you're like this?" His voice sounded thick and gravelly.

She sauntered over to him.

"Is this how we're going to ratify a peace treaty?" He asked. *Don't look down at her breasts.* This was supposed to be a serious conversation. *Just one kiss below her belly button.*

"How do you want to open negotiations?" She folded her hands over her breasts, but the gesture teased him with a peek at nipples like chocolate-dipped tips.

"I don't want to do this anymore." He uttered his protest with a growl. He took a few seconds to get his thoughts straight. Probably should have finessed that much better.

"But neither do I."

"I don't want to settle for drive-by sex." Although he had no complaints with the delivery.

"Neither do I."

"I'm not a casual acquaintance," he clarified.

Desire oozed off her body. His body answered. He was hard and waiting for the green light. But he wasn't going to back down from what he had to say. "Once, three years ago, I said that I loved you and you shut me down, then you shut me out. I'm going to take the risk again because this is who I am—a man in love. And I love you, Fiona Reed. I want you in my life, every day, every night. No platonic-partner BS."

She didn't respond with any ready quips. The seductive smile disappeared into a thoughtful countenance.

Leo tried to read the body signals and expressions. But she stood with such solemnity that he feared he'd pushed too hard. He'd failed.

"I came over tonight to tell you that I am not going to live my life hiding from the truth."

He clasped her face with his hands and gently kissed her forehead.

"Although I've said this in my heart, in my private moments away from you, I have loved you from the beginning. I do really love you, Leo Starks."

"We're on the same footing," he said with conviction.

She nodded. "I think we're talking too much now. Don't you?" Her smile invited, drew him like a starving man to sustenance. "Kiss me."

"No problem." He offered the solution that his body craved. His mouth lowered and reclaimed the softness of her mouth.

Their fusion sparked energy, bold and hot.

The tray of food remained abandoned on the counter. He lifted her, cupping her behind, and effortlessly carried her to the bedroom. Her legs wound around his hips to seal their bodies together.

Leo couldn't stop kissing her. The plumpness of her lips seduced him, taunting his tongue with their fullness. Gently, he lowered her to the bed, where she stretched out into a graceful curve with her arms overhead. His appreciative gaze bathed the length of her body as he put on the condom.

Her naked body, brown skin and all, was natural and beautiful. She twisted her torso, teasing him with poses. Her hand beckoned him to come to her, over her. "What are you thinking about?" she asked with a dreamy smile.

"How lucky I am." He straddled her legs, deliberately lowering himself to brush against the moist slit of her sex.

She wiggled under him, rubbing her hips against his hardness. "Then let's celebrate."

Leo didn't need to be told another time. His hands grasped her behind to raise her hips like a sexy gift for his arousal.

Taking his time, he entered her wetness. The sensation rendered him speechless. His eyes squeezed shut as he pumped slowly. His grunts mixed with Fiona's hissing every time he pushed in. Their enjoyment was in sync.

Her legs locked him into place. He didn't want to be anywhere but firmly between her legs. She ran her fingernails against the sides of his thighs, driving him crazy. Her hips bucked against him, setting the pace for their act. They rose and fell together, alternating between the hard, frenetic grind and a slow, languorous slide in and out of her sex.

Sweat slicked their bodies. And his chest scoured her breasts. Her nipples beaded and pressed against his sensitive skin. Every part of him was aroused in equal response to her body's reaction.

Her body quivered its call.

He answered with his thrusts.

Their harmony was sealed in the tangled sheets, fueled by their sweat and fused in their passions. Every tremor of her desire welling along his shaft, sending its message, was a private invitation for his arousal.

She moaned.

He grunted.

His hand cupped her breast, fingers tweaking her nipples. He loved stirring the gasps and soft grunts that escaped from her mouth. Then he covered her responses with his mouth, letting them sink and settle into him. They gave him energy.

Their sensual, erotic beat shifted into higher gear.

The point of no return. He wanted to send her to the stratosphere.

Leo eased out of her, then placed his mouth where he'd just filled her. In one quick swoop, he bathed her with his tongue, tasting her sweetness. Flicking her clit with the tip of his tongue, he teased her into a frenzy. Her sex was swollen and wet. The lips were tender to the lashes of his tongue. He blew at the clit before stroking it with long laps. She was on the edge. The same point where he already stood, poised for their leap together.

"Baby, are you ready…?" Sheer ecstasy ramped up, on a fierce boil, ready to tip over for a full release.

"Anytime…for you…baby." She snapped him between her thighs.

The fuse was lit. The fire increased, blazing to a sensual inferno. Together they ran, soared, flying out to nowhere, and yet it felt like they were all-powerful and everywhere.

Their guttural cries mixed and mingled to the cadence of their writhing limbs. He could feel her climax, his arousal stroked by her quivering walls.

Leo swore as his body released like a powerful jet.

"I don't want to float back down," Fiona whispered in his ear.

"We can lift off again."

"Soon. I hope."

"I might have a heart attack, but I'm ready—" Leo could barely talk.

"And I'm willing."

They shared a gentle kiss before settling, clasped in each other's arms. Their journey had been a long one, sometimes difficult, sometimes unpredictable, but every bit had been worth it.

He had his woman.

She had his heart.

They would be together forever.

* * * * *

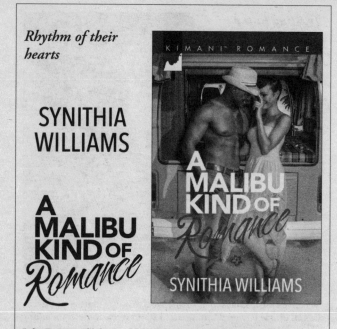

REQUEST YOUR FREE BOOKS!

2 FREE NOVELS
PLUS 2 FREE GIFTS!

KIMANI™
ROMANCE

Love's ultimate destination!

*In med school, Felicia Blake couldn't help being
impressed by Griffin Kaile's physique, as well as his
intellect. The youngest of the accomplished Blake
triplets, Felicia put aside dating to focus on her
career. She may have fantasized about Griffin, but not
about discovering that he's the biological father of
the baby girl she's been asked to raise. Felicia is the
most stunning woman Griffin has ever known. Now
that the daughter he never knew about has brought
them together, he's eager to explore their romantic
potential. But ambitious Felicia is reluctant to jump
from passion to instant family. Which leaves Griffin
only one choice—to somehow show her that this kind of
breathtaking chemistry occurs only once in a lifetime...*

*Read on for a sneak peek at
TEMPTING THE HEIRESS, the next exciting
installment in author Martha Kennerson's
THE BLAKE SISTERS series!*

"Dr. Griffin Kaile," Felicia said, pulling herself together.
"It's been a while."

"Yes, it has, and you haven't changed a bit. You look
amazing," he said, smiling.

Felicia looked down at her outfit and frowned. "Not
really, but thanks. You look...professional."

Griffin smirked. "Thanks."

Professional. Really, Felicia? "How have you been?" she asked, breaking eye contact when she spied the gift from her sisters—red Valextra Avietta luggage—making its way down the carousel's runway. Felicia reached for the large wheeled trolley.

"I got it," Griffin said, placing his hand over hers.

Griffin's touch sent a charge through her body that she'd only felt one other time before, delivered by the same man. Felicia quickly pulled her hand from his and took a step back. "I'm doing well." Griffin picked up the large bag and placed it next to Felicia before reaching for his own leather suitcase.

"What a gentleman," Felicia heard a woman say.

"Thanks," Felicia said, smiling up at him.

"Last I heard, you were working somewhere overseas," Griffin said.

Felicia nodded. "I've spent the past year working in Asia."

"Wow, I bet that was an adventure. Are you in town long? We should get together…catch up," Griffin suggested, the corner of his mouth rising slowly.

"I…I'd really like that, but I'm only in town for the day. Unexpected and urgent business I have to tend to."

"I can't convince you to extend your trip?" Griffin asked, offering her a wide smile.

Don't miss TEMPTING THE HEIRESS
by Martha Kennerson, available September 2016
wherever Harlequin® Kimani Romance™
books and ebooks are sold!